The Virtues of Hell

The Virtues of Hell

Pierre Boulle

Translation by Patricia Wolf

CASSELL · LONDON

CASSELL & COMPANY LTD
an imprint of
Cassell & Collier Macmillan Publishers Ltd
35 Red Lion Square, London WC1R 4SG
and at Sydney, Auckland, Toronto, Johannesburg

and an affiliate of The Macmillan Company Inc, New York

First published as *Les Vertus de l'enfer*, 1974
First published in Great Britain 1975

ISBN 0 304 29539 6

Printed in Great Britain by
The Camelot Press Ltd, Southampton
F. 1274

". . . perhaps not a very common type, but I can safely assure my readers that he is not the product of coldly distorted thinking."

JOSEPH CONRAD

Part One

1

BUTLER TRIED TO steady his trembling hand by pressing hard against his side with his forearm, at the end of which projected a gun. He had learned that technique in a special combat-training course prior to his service in Vietnam. The act he was about to perform terrified him. Necessity alone drove him to it: the compelling need for drug.

The New York neighborhood he had singled out after careful deliberation was deserted now. Respectable folk headed homeward from the movies or the theater; night people still crowded the bars. From behind the street corner, he peered out one last time to make certain that the approaching pedestrian was alone and his own path of retreat clear.

"Stop where you are and toss me your billfold!"

Words common enough to appear almost daily in the press, which invariably advised any passer-by so accosted to comply without argument. Butler managed to master his trepidation long enough to articulate them, advancing with hopefully menacing strides, pointing the gun with a hand that never stopped shaking despite his efforts to contract the muscles.

His voice ringing out in the dark stillness magnified his fears. The words he had forced himself to shout, words he

3

had repeated over and over for hours, sounded ludicrous and incongruous coming from his own mouth.

The man stopped, undismayed. He said nothing —merely eyed Butler as if trying to measure his resolve from the look in his eye. There was barely enough light in the street to distinguish faces but Butler felt that his ashen features stood out glaringly in the darkness. He was sorry not to have worn a mask as movie gangsters do.

The silence dragged on. The man continued to observe him without saying a word. Butler felt an urge to turn and run, but got a grip on himself. "Did you hear me? Toss over your billfold or else. . . ."

The dryness in his throat made the words sound peculiar. The man seemed to be smiling as if it were all something of a joke. At last he spoke, pointing calmly, steadily, at the weapon. "Is it loaded?"

"Of course."

"You know how to use it?"

"Just try me!"

A supreme effort to act like a desperado; yet the contrast between the man's firm, even voice and his own flustered stammer began to unsettle him.

"Are you sure it's my wallet you want?" the man asked with a tinge of sarcasm. "I hate to give it up; I really need some of the papers in it and they're useless to you. Won't you take money instead?"

"All right."

The man's smile seemed to broaden at this hasty acceptance of his offer. "How much?"

"Fifty dollars."

"Thirty."

"All right."

Ignominious surrender. The man drew out his wallet, counted the bills in a leisurely fashion, and held them out.

4

Butler hesitated, then stepped forward, still pointing the ridiculous gun. He snatched the money with fingers so unsteady that one of the bills fluttered to the ground. Instead of picking it up, he retreated quickly, as if fearing a trap. He guessed that the man could disarm him if he tried. But that was not the stranger's intent and he made no such move. Butler glanced nervously over his shoulder, prepared to flee.

"Wait a minute!"

The voice was commanding, and, at the same time, vaguely sympathetic. Not for a minute did it occur to him to challenge the authority of the man, now approaching and observing him at close range with mounting interest.

"Hooked on drugs?"

Without a trace of defiance, Butler simply nodded his head.

"I thought so.... Don't be afraid; addicts are my friends.... Heroin?"

"Heroin."

"And you're on your last legs, right? You need the money for a fix or two, right?"

"I've got to have it, tonight." He felt as if subjected to the interrogation of a superior, and always in the presence of such persons his will weakened. During the detoxification treatment he underwent in Vietnam, he responded readily, not to say obsequiously, to the psychiatrist's questions, impressed as much by the latter's professional status as by his military rank.

The stranger thought a moment, then made a decision. "Come with me. Let's have a little talk. Maybe I can help you out. First, though, put that plaything back in your pocket.... It's not loaded, is it?"

"No, not loaded," Butler stammered, doing as he was bid.

5

"I thought so," said the man, taking his arm. "Trust me. I'm not going to ask for the money back. You earned it—it's yours. I may be able to do something else for you, like get you what you need for nothing. But I must get to know you better first. All I ask is that you answer my questions honestly. It's strictly between the two of us. Are you up to it now? I mean—do you have to have a needle right away?"

A change in Butler's expression prompted the question. A strained look crept over his face; his body shuddered, not from fear this time. He managed to control himself. The stranger's presence and remarks seemed to affect him like a tranquilizer. This benevolent authority, threatening at first, gave him a moment's peace. He felt instinctively trustful, a rare state of mind for him. He could have counted on the fingers of one hand the times he had sensed a sympathetic vibration in others. He never made much effort to respond to such sympathy, and when he did almost always failed.

Tonight, with this man who had reacted so paradoxically to his pitiable attempt at holdup, he felt an urge to pursue the acquaintance. The man didn't appear to be lying; having known from the outset that the gun wasn't loaded, he had done nothing about it and in fact had gone along with the act and handed over his money. That gesture alone deserved thanks and at least an effort to prolong the conversation despite the gnawing torment that was beginning to plague him. Straightening himself up, he declared firmly, "I need a fix but I can wait. I'll answer your questions."

The man nodded approvingly. "Good. Chalk one up for you. I'll wager you haven't reached the critical stage. What's your name?"

"Butler. John Butler."

"Come along, Butler . . . and don't be afraid of me. I tell you that addicts are my friends."

2

"INDIVIDUALLY, DOCTOR, HE doesn't interest me," said
Stephens, "but he has connections with a suspected
member of a very powerful dealer organization. . . a cagey
operator, that guy, never sticks his neck out. We've been
watching him for months, unable to pin him down or uncover a shred of evidence. He isn't the top man, though he's
fairly high up, I think. . . . As for this Butler fellow, he
seems to belong to the depressing herd of hardened addicts
that you know all about. Ready to do anything short of an
honest day's work to obtain that vital daily fix, they become
tools of hoodlums who use them as pushers. There are hundreds like him in New York. . ."

Dr. Edmund interrupted. "Butler? Did you say Butler?
John Butler?"

"That's the one. . . . A classic case and probably only a
tiny cog in the wheel, but his contact with the other man
caught our attention and I'd like to know more about him.
He's a veteran who got on drugs in Vietnam, then took the
cure prior to discharge. So he must have been one of your
patients. I see his name rings a bell."

"I remember him indeed; I'll tell you why in a moment. Go on."

A former army psychiatrist, Dr. Edmund had run a drug

clinic in Cat Thai, near Saigon, organized in 1970 to combat an alarming rise in drug abuse among the expeditionary forces. He left the army after the war to open a similar private clinic in New York and to manage a rehabilitation center for former addicts.

From time to time, he also acted as a medical consultant to the Bureau of Narcotics and Dangerous Drugs. Stephens, a top man in the Bureau, had come to consult him that evening as he was in the habit of doing whenever in need of information about veterans who had undergone treatment at Cat Thai. The Bureau had files on most of them, but Dr. Edmund kept a store of private notes which he released only if they could help the agency. Stephens valued the doctor's experience and often gained insights from him into the mental and behavioral patterns of King Drug's unfortunate subjects who were frequently in touch with dealers.

"I don't know too much about him—a poor soldier, according to his officers, though he volunteered for Vietnam after induction; not a strong-willed fellow, far from it; a great malingerer. Sheer cowardice on one occasion, deserving of severe punishment, though my records aren't complete and I have no details on the incident."

"I do," murmured the doctor.

"He spent a little over a year in Vietnam and probably began taking drugs at some intermediate point. Heroin —condition not irreversible, but headed that way. Volunteered for treatment in your clinic. Sent home afterwards. That's it, except, as I told you, he's been seen lately hanging around with a suspicious person who may be in the pay of an important dealer."

"I can add a bit more," the doctor began slowly. "The reason I remember him so well is, first of all, because I took notes on him over there. . . . Not that he was an exceptional

8

case; far from it. Dozens of times I was tempted to hand him over to one of my assistants."

Stephens smiled. Edmund had a reputation for grabbing the extraordinary patients and shunting smaller fry onto his subordinates.

"As a matter of fact, he was a typical addict. Irresolute, unambitious, unaggressive, unsociable. Still, there were some interesting facets to his personality. . . . I know him well chiefly because I treated him a second time here in New York, about a year ago."

"Same problem?"

"Yes. And after the cure had its usual effects I put him in my rehabilitation facility where people like him are kept under observation by professionals who try to prepare them to resume a normal life in society."

"So he had a relapse after leaving you?"

"Shortly afterwards. . . . And now you tell me. . ."

"It's quite probable."

"I'm not surprised," the doctor sighed.

"Would you call him a hopeless case?"

Edmund merely grimaced sourly, then got up and walked over to a file containing private notes for a scientific study he intended to publish. He removed a folder and opened it. "I have extensive notes on the man. His second treatment enabled me to fill in the gaps in our earlier talks."

"You psychoanalyzed him?"

"That word is meaningless. We had a series of talks and I tried to win his confidence in order to advise him more effectively. I did the same for all those poor fellows when I could spare the time, because moral support means more to them than medical care. In Butler's case, I had the impression, at one point, that I was succeeding and could even cure him permanently. But there wasn't enough time. . . . Detoxification is easy, Stephens, at least for those who

9

haven't reached the point of no return, like him. The treatment almost always works, but it isn't enough. I did everything I could for him and the others. They were in pretty good shape by the time they left my clinic at Caï Thai, and I warned them, I told them. . ."

Stephens knew by heart what the psychiatrist advised his patients but that it was useless to try to interrupt him when he got onto this subject. Better just listen and return to the point later on.

". . . I told all of them and I told him, too—the treatment you've just successfully undergone, is a mere fraction of your rehabilitation. You now need psychological therapy, and for that you must act as your own doctors. It is imperative that you search for and find an *interest* in life, an outside interest to take your mind off yourselves. You must seek out an environment in which you feel at ease—such an environment exists for all of us—and make the effort to adapt to it even if you initially meet rejection. . . .

"That, Stephens, is what all of them lack—an environment in which to breathe freely, social contacts, friends whose sympathy and guidance they can rely on. The absence of such a climate is what drives them back to the insidious lure of demon drugs, which, in the beginning, create the illusion of a relaxing atmosphere. Experience has taught me this—whenever a permanent cure is achieved—and the instances are fairly rare. . ."

"Ten percent, I think," Stephens observed matter-of-factly.

"About ten percent; that's very few, I admit. . . . Well, in all such cases the patient had discovered the moral support he needed and was never able to find. . . . I mentioned the need for an outside interest which can take any number of forms. For many it's a woman; not a passionate love affair—they're incapable of it—but a strong-minded woman

10

who can dominate without their knowing it, for the majority of them are children.... A woman, or a male friend, or simply a job in pleasant surroundings. Then gradually they emerge from their mental cocoon, gradually they accustom themselves to the idea of action and become capable of acting.... For action and initiative, Stephens, are the criteria for a permanent cure."

"The symptoms of permanent rehabilitation, perhaps, but not the road to it, I think," Stephens murmured skeptically. "Making war didn't exactly appeal to Butler and a few others."

"One form of action unsuited to his temperament, that's all.... But if you read some of these cases..." His fingers flipped over the row of folders in the drawer like a deck of cards with the possessiveness of a collector displaying his rare pieces. "Here's one who was cured by a passion for money. Messenger boy in a stockbrokerage firm—about the only job he could perform, and not too brilliantly at that—he started out by investing a small amount on his own. It mushroomed. He went on doing this and gradually built up a tidy fortune; it absorbed him and brought him such satisfaction that he quit drugs altogether.... And here's a case that's even odder. A man who renounced heroin and became a slave to poker. Yes, this new passion demanded constant self-control for he actually became a first-class sharper."

"Your cured addicts don't appear to adopt a very strict standard of morality, Doctor," Stephens commented drily, "but I don't suppose you counsel them in these directions."

"I avoid giving specific advice; they must find their own tools for survival. But if I knew for certain, Stephens, that a particular vice would get them off drugs, I wouldn't hesitate to prescribe it. There is no more destructive demon than heroin.... I've only mentioned the most extreme

11

cases, the most interesting ones from my point of view. Your motives, of course, are different. Now as far as this Butler is concerned. . ."

"I gather that you made the same recommendations to him after his second cure and repeated them when he was in your other facility—what's the name of it?"

"It has no name. You can call it psychological rehabilitation moral regeneration. . . . No, I had no chance to do it then," the doctor added tartly, "as he left the center after three days."

"You let him go?"

"He simply disappeared. Took to his heels, you might say. Anyway, I couldn't have stopped him. He was a free agent, the treatment was voluntary."

"How do you explain his relapse?"

"I wish I could!" the doctor exclaimed with sudden animation. "He ran off one evening, I tell you, without a word to anyone, after only three days. Maybe he didn't like the center though my assistants and the whole staff did their best to create a warm, friendly atmosphere—nothing like a mental institution or a hospital, and a far cry from a prison. No surveillance, or practically none—witness the results! Games, sports, entertainment, contests. No nurses, only companions, sympathetic counselors—those are my orders and they are strictly carried out. But all this didn't seem to help him, Stephens. He couldn't find the support he needed. Sometimes I feel almost guilty about it."

"Did you make any prognosis after that?"

"My notes end with a large question mark with a pessimistic diaeresis below, a symbol I invented. His history allows few grounds for optimism and points to complete absence of will, a very alarming factor."

"Tell me something about his past."

Stephens had dropped by routinely, not expecting to

learn anything terribly sensational about this queer fellow Butler. He had come simply because he felt it incumbent on him to pursue every lead involving persons connected with the drug world. Once in a while, however, and that day was such a time, he discovered a broader human interest in the psychiatrist's remarks. Later he would sift out whatever might prove useful to the Narcotics Bureau.

"Concerning the period he served in Vietnam, I can simply confirm what you know: he was a terrible soldier. The incident you mentioned might have led to a court-martial but for the fact that the impending cease-fire had produced a certain laxity in military discipline at all levels. Would you like to hear what he told me about it?... an unsolicited confession of sorts... without any attempt to minimize his failings—as if he knew no other way to behave. A prime example of what you would call cowardice, though we psychiatrists..."

Before the doctor could digress on a scientific tangent, Stephens urged him to come to the point. He was anxious now to develop some solid information for the files.

3

... The patrol had been advancing since daybreak in a sector known to be dangerous. Heavy overcast, clouds merging with mist rising from the forest frequently obscured the treetops. You have to have experienced it to understand, Doctor. . . . Those hostile mountains in the highlands during the rainy season when fog rots the jungle. Sinister, I tell you. Not a breath of air, not a birdcall. Only the panting of weary men. . . But I wasn't tired, Doctor, I was simply scared to death. I couldn't feel another thing.

"And, in fact, Stephens, fear dominated his whole story—relentless fear, admitted freely, almost boastingly, at times."

Hunched over his file, Dr. Edmund was reading the account of Butler's story that he had written from memory based on the soldier's own words. He interrupted his reading regularly to add details he hadn't bothered to write down but which came to mind as he recalled the incident.

"Shipped out to Vietnam a few months before, it was the first such scouting party he had gone on. Up till then he had been assigned to a unit in the Saigon district and had

14

never ventured outside the city limits or been exposed to anything worse than sporadic mortar fire. Being suddenly thrust into the jungle was enough, certainly, to churn up deep anxieties... intensifying the effect of the stories he had heard in camp. He told me some of those nightmarish tales—not all of them fiction—that circulated around the barracks after dark. Stories about traps concealed in the underbrush, mines ready to explode at the foot of every tree, deep pits hidden under piles of branches to snare scouts and impale them on sharp spikes, poisoned arrows, and who knows what else... I can understand why he called the setting sinister. A dreadful sense of helplessness... panic-stricken by every mound of earth, afraid to set his foot down.

"But on top of that, the human atmosphere was equally odious to him. Listen to his description of the sergeant in charge of the patrol."

> ...He was a mean brute, a sadist who delighted in terrifying me.... "With this damn fog," he was always complaining, "I can scream my lungs out for air support if Charlie shows his face. They'd let us all croak before sending a single helicopter into this pea soup. I warn you, you'll have no one but yourselves to rely on if we're attacked, and from what I've seen of Charlie, he'll attack whenever he can. A day like today is just what Charlie ordered. You'd better not chicken out."... The remarks were meant for me in particular. He knew I was paralyzed with fear; I couldn't hide it from him.

"For you and everyone else, I pointed out. But he wouldn't listen; he was convinced that the sergeant was talking only to him."

15

. . .To me only, Doctor, I can assure you. He was always eyeing me with a nasty, sneering look. He despised me, and whenever we were sent on a particularly dangerous patrol—say to a rice field in the mountains where you lurch along narrow embankments, unprotected, without even a tree to duck behind, a perfect target for snipers in the surrounding hills—he always stuck me at the head of the column. I tell you he hated me. . . . And the other fellows, the veterans, they snickered too when they saw me quaking.

"I suppose you'd call that a persecution complex," Stephens commented.

"Of course, another classic symptom, too easily interpreted. From all Butler's complaints I gathered that the sergeant was a tough old bird who made it his practice to put newcomers on their guard. Half his men were raw recruits like Butler; that situation was common at the time. The ranks of experienced fighters were thinning out and being replaced with whatever was available. My impression of the sergeant was confirmed later by one of his commanding officers—he wasn't the bully described by Butler. Tough, yes, an ex-marine covered with scars and decorations who had done his stint in Korea, then Vietnam, where he developed expert knowledge of the country and the enemy; strict, but intelligent and not the type who would indulge in pointless ragging, especially in a danger zone. A sense of responsibility made him talk that way, not just to Butler but to everyone. As for the others laughing at him, you can be sure they didn't have time to watch and sneer at him on perilous missions. . . . It's a familiar tale; he simply couldn't adjust to the environment.

"Picture him as I do in that hostile country. . . in that

dank, sodden, fogbound forest studded with unseen dangers which his imagination balloons into greater and more mysterious perils, surrounded by trailmates he looks upon as enemies. . . No point reading you all this," Dr. Edmund went on, impatiently thumbing through several pages. "You get the same sense of fear and anguish. Now he comes to the incident you mentioned."

> . . . We'd been marching for hours, eyes peeled for danger. Shortly after noon we arrived at our destination—the crest of a hill approached by a narrow path barely wide enough for one vehicle, over which a convoy of three trucks was due to pass with arms and ammunition for a South Vietnamese outpost. The beleaguered garrison, in a Vietcong-infested region and subject to nightly attacks, was in desperate need of supplies. . . . At least that's how Sanders explained it before we left; I wasn't paying attention to such trivial details. . . .

"Sanders, of course, was the bugbearish sergeant," Edmund explained.

> . . . We marched ahead like scouts, combing the woods on either side of the trail. Our orders were to camp at the top of the hill, an especially risky spot, and protect the convoy from possible ambush. Other patrols had been sent ahead, I think, to do likewise.
>
> As usual, Sanders harped on the dangerous terrain and the probability of attack. The moment we arrived he began grumbling about how crazy it was to send a lightly-armed party into such a deathtrap. The patrol numbered twenty men, with

17

three Lewis machine-guns. Surrounded by the jungle... impenetrable in the vicinity of the hillside, Doctor. Up to there we could at least move through it, but to reach the crest we had to stay on the trail. .... a wall of branches and tangled vines without a pathway or the tiniest opening—for us, that is, though I expected at any moment to see hordes of Vietcong, who know their way blindfold in the brush, come pouring out from behind this wall.

The sergeant did his best to investigate the area with a handful of men, including myself, naturally! We didn't get far. He gave up, cursing. We found ourselves up to our necks in a maze of thorny, spiny plants that cut like knife blades. Returning to the trail, the sergeant set up the three machine-guns fairly close together to cover the convoy route up the hillside. The rest of us were to protect the gunners from a rear-end attack out of the jungle. I was in one of those groups... four or five men with M-16 rifles who couldn't see more than three yards ahead. The sergeant posted himself farther away, near another machine-gun.

After a long, nerve-racking wait, I finally heard the trucks approaching; ... then came another seemingly endless pause. At last they appeared, escorted by two light tanks, looming out of the fog like phantoms, almost on top of us, winding up the hill in a roar of engines. Then the attack came.

The two tanks were hit first. ... The shells must have come from the surrounding hills beyond the trail. The tanks exploded. .. clouds of black smoke. I remember the crews writhing in flames on the ground while a Vietcong commando unit swooped out of the hills and rushed for the trucks, screaming like madmen. They wanted the arms and ammunition. . . .

"He seems to have recalled every detail," Stephens commented.

"Yes, I doubt that he'll ever forget the scene. It must have been pretty grim. Other servicemen were ambushed in the jungles of Vietnam—but, fortunately, not all of them were as sensitive as he or reacted the way he did."

"He ran?"

"At the first shot. Listen."

. . . The sergeant shouted a command and the machine-guns opened up. Just at that moment another Vietcong unit attacked us from behind. They had probably been waiting there for hours, unwilling to make a move for fear of alerting the convoy. The first shots killed one man in my group. The others returned fire. . . . I couldn't do it, Doctor; caught in a crossfire, don't you see? . . . And there were so many of them, pouring out from behind every tree. One was approaching me; I knew it, I saw the underbrush parting. . . . I hurled my rifle as hard as I could in his direction. . . . Yes, I thought it would stop him somehow, that he might spare my life. . . . I did it and ran without so much as a glance behind me. I heard the sergeant screaming and cursing me; he was heading our way just then and saw me. . .

"That's the story he told me in Cat Thai, Stephens, without any encouragement on my part."

"I see," said Stephens after a pause. "Others were court-martialed for such acts."

"No one knew the facts at the time, it seems. The convoy fell into enemy hands; such things occurred every day. The entire patrol was killed or captured; there were no witnesses. Sergeant Sanders was wounded and taken prisoner, but I found out that he survived and managed to escape a few months later, towards the end of the war; a tough soldier, that man. The whole episode had been forgotten. He didn't feel like reviving it, or if he tried to, was put off with another piece of hardware to pin on his chest. . . . When Butler finally rejoined his unit after wandering for two days in the jungle, he wasn't in a boasting mood. He told them he had been captured along with the others and escaped during the night. They believed him, . . . or more likely, they pretended to believe him. No fuss, no scandal—that was military policy in those days."

"Still, it's odd that he should tell you all that. Cowards generally don't boast about their cowardice."

"It was probably compulsive. . . a kind of confession. Or perhaps remorse. Besides, up to then he trusted me."

"And afterwards?"

"As I said, he ran away from my center."

Stephens thought a moment. Though the story was of no real use to him at the time, he made mental notes of it, all the same, emphasizing Butler's psychological quirks which might prove of use to him later when dealing with other individuals. "You spoke of remorse," he said finally, "and if those were actually his words you took down, then in fact I do sense that kind of feeling in him. . . . A feeling stronger than regret, a profound distress at having conducted himself so badly."

20

"True, and that's what led me to hope for a while that he might be saved."

"Perhaps the episode was the result of the kind of momentary lapse that can happen to anyone under certain conditions."

The doctor shook his head skeptically. "It would be a mistake, Stephens, to see him as another Lord Jim. His entire war record in Vietnam is fairly unwholesome, and if you care to hear about his civilian career, you'll agree with me that Captain Marlow could never have felt any spiritual kinship with him."

An avid reader, Dr. Edmund lost no occasion to cite his favorite writers. Among them was Conrad whose books he considered immensely interesting to psychiatry.

"Let's not digress," said Stephens, grinning. "He interests me because of his possible connection with an organization I'm fighting, the worst criminals we know. . . . Do you know when he began taking drugs?"

"You can assume that it was shortly after this incident. Cheap and easy to come by over there. Others did the same thing."

It was in fact easy. In Saigon, in Da Nang, in Hué, a dose of refined heroin cost two or three dollars and was available in any bar. Once rare in Indochina, the use of heroin mushroomed in Vietnam from the war and from fear. Colonials and natives alike had formerly derived their escapist pleasures from opium pipes, but opium proved powerless to dispel the horrors of jungle warfare or the memory of atrocities. A more potent narcotic was needed.

Butler and many others followed the same pattern. A girl he picked up in Saigon introduced him to the drug and showed him how to inject it. A second shot followed, and with it, a growing dependence. For a while he tried to put off using the drug until just before leaving on patrol, the worst ordeal of all. Soon, however, on his return from those missions, assailed by thoughts of real and imaginary perils, he got into the habit of using the needle regularly.

"You'll say that he had good cause," concluded the doctor, "and I can't disagree, he and many others. A singularly loathsome war in hostile surroundings, a sense of rootlessness, a debilitating climate and, as if that weren't enough, constant temptation. . . an army of petty pushers, prostitutes, and pimps, eager to make money selling a product that major Chinese dealers had begun to stockpile when the arrival of the Americans was first announced. Maybe Butler would never have gotten hooked if he had had to go out and obtain the stuff for himself. Still. . ."

"What?"

"On second thought, I believe he was destined to do what he did. His personality made him an ideal victim for the demon heroin."

"His personality?"

"I'm afraid the rest of his story doesn't improve his image. He was just as cowardly in civilian life as in the army. . . . A jellyfish, to some; to me, simply a pathological case of mental instability that would have taken years of treatment to cure."

"Tell me about his background. Not an exciting topic, I gather."

"Exciting, Stephens? . . . Good Lord, a chronicle so banal and dull that it's sickening!"

4

BUTLER'S CHILDHOOD LOOMED as a glaring illustration of the banality deplored by Dr. Edmund. He recited it hastily in a monotonous, faintly irritated voice, as if annoyed at himself for taking the time to enunciate such commonplaces. The influences on Butler's character formation were so obvious to the psychiatrist that he resented having to dwell on them.

> . . . Parents didn't get along; daily quarrels; mother increasingly absent from home; finally killed in an automobile accident when he was still quite young. Father paid scant attention to him except to register displeasure at his poor marks in school.

"Well, I warned you that it was one long platitude: a childhood totally devoid of warmth and affection. Unfortunately, this type of platitude is also pernicious."

> Nor did adolescence improve the picture much for Butler. With an inferior record in high school, he was admitted to college through his father's influence and couldn't adjust to that either.

"His own fault, certainly; he was unsociable."

Studying bored him. He had an instinctive aversion to learning, hated every course he took, and lacked the stimulus or imagination to look for subjects to arouse his interest. After various psychological tests had disclosed a singularly passive temperament, anguished confusion in response to the realities of life, and hostile indifference to action, his advisers steered him, quite understandably, toward the humanities. And with lamentable results: he fell asleep over the classics and his papers were cited as prime examples of cliché-ridden trivia. His grades sank so low that he was expelled at the end of the term.

His father lectured him severely, then used his influence again (he was a prominent figure in the chemical industry) to gain him admission to a chemical engineering college. All he asked of the boy was that he exert a minimum of conscientious effort in order to earn his diploma and be assured of a livelihood.

Even that was beyond him. College science courses held no more appeal than literature. Chemistry, with its host of diabolical formulae (the expression was his), seemed monstrous. In no time it became evident that he would never master its fundamentals—let alone acquire enough skill to hold down even a modest job as laboratory assistant. His father then delivered an even stiffer lecture than before, with no apparent effect other than to reinforce the boy's notion that he would always be a failure.

"Not very charitable of him, though it seems he was justified," Stephens observed.

"Maybe so, but ill-advised and probably harmful from

a medical standpoint."

"I see. Did he have any outside interests?"

"That's the tragic part, Stephens—he had none at all. At least none that came out in our sessions together."

> Butler showed no interest in sports either. Not that he lacked the physique, for in fact he had a sturdy build and could run, jump, and put the shot as well as the next man, and proved it in several athletic meets when he first entered college. And yet, he hated to train. Soon he gave up even trying to compete and allowed himself to be beaten by inferior athletes. He disliked team sports most of all, and eventually, because of his poor sportsmanship, none of the players would have him on their side.

"Though secretly relieved by this, I think, he took it as a rejection. He wasn't very popular, needless to say. He seems not to have had a single friend; I can understand how the others reacted to him. A poor student and poor friend, they must have felt, at least that's my impression from the little he told me about them, expressing much the same feeling that he did in describing the sergeant. He thought they hated him and made a practice of excluding him from their fun and activities."

"A persecution complex. You were right, Doctor; that's hardly the way I'd want my son to turn out. . . . How about sex?"

"He never said much about it. I assume he's normal, if that's what you mean, but I doubt that he's found much pleasure in it. Sex, like everything else, seems not to have inspired him. His experiences left him disillusioned and bewildered. You can also assume that such a man doesn't arouse much of a response in women."

"Was he drafted and shipped off to Vietnam after

expulsion from college?"

"Not right away."

> . . . Discouraged, and convinced by teachers' re-
> ports that his son would never be able to find a
> proper place for himself in the world, Butler's
> father got him a very ordinary job in a third-rate
> business firm, work involving no initiative or ef-
> fort. Reading, writing, and simple arithmetic were
> the only skills required.

"All he had to do, for a small salary, of course, was to
keep files and add up sales. Most modern businesses do this
by machine. Well, here again, as he admitted shamelessly
to me, the results were disastrous. Filing cards got lost; his
addition was full of mistakes. For lack of disciplined effort,
he managed once again to get himself fired."

> At that point, his father gave up and left him to his
> own devices, arranging to send him a monthly pit-
> tance barely sufficient to keep him from starving,
> which he might well have done in view of his
> inability to earn a living.
> Butler decided to try a change of environment
> and began to frequent hippie circles, not drug ad-
> dicts—drugs hadn't yet entered his life—but genu-
> ine hippies. That didn't work out either, for the
> hippies also rejected him. Then the draft caught
> him and he volunteered to serve in Vietnam.

"The rest you know."

"Curious, this volunteering for a combat zone. A young
fellow who was scared of his own shadow."

"Another factor that once made me think he wasn't a

hopeless case. It was probably part of his search for a new environment, something different from what he had grown up in. Perhaps he imagined a world of exciting adventures where he could at last fit in. If that was his dream, he deluded himself cruelly."

"So cruelly that drugs provided the only resort? Inevitable moral decay in my opinion, Doctor. Don't you agree?"

Dr. Edmund arched one eyebrow, a mannerism he used to express surprise or profound reflection. "It's always hard for me to make such a diagnosis. After all, each of these individuals is a separate case. Each may possess hidden resources which some surprising combination of circumstances could bring out. But from what I know of drug addicts, and judging from his history of relapses and disappearances, I honestly can't see what could possibly save him from heroin."

"Neither can I," said Stephens, getting up. "As I see it, he has already or will fall into the hands of some powerful gang of criminals who will dole out his daily ration of poison in return for a few simple services, such as selling on the streets, one of the few things he's capable of doing. That will continue, along with ever-increasing doses, until he reaches the stage when he can no longer perform his grim little chore. Then the gang will turn him out or else liquidate him. He'll go off and hang himself or take one last, lethal dose, if he still has enough drugs to do it."

"I'm afraid you're too good a prophet," the doctor murmured. "Lots of them end up that way. Another cliché."

Stephens shook his head emphatically. "It's really none of my business, Doctor. My job is to follow a trail that starts with insignificant fellows like him and leads to the source of the evil: the big game. It's hard, it takes months, sometimes years, but we do succeed. Thanks for filling me in. I'll let you know if I hear anything about him."

27

5

"I'VE TAKEN ON a new fellow for the sales staff," Herrick reported.

"An addict?" Fitz's question was purely rhetorical as Herrick hired only addicts for that kind of work.

"An addict, at the end of his rope, reduced to robbing at gunpoint for the few dollars he needs to maintain his habit."

"Which brings your total sales force to . . . ?"

Herrick supplied the number instantly. Taking a notebook out of his pocket, Fitz nodded approval at the penciled figure he read, erased it, and entered the new one. He insisted on being informed immediately of any change in his staff, but this was the only record he kept, a written count of his salesmen, the lowest category of his personnel—an isolated number that could mean anything. Higher-level, international operations were handled by a more elaborate bookkeeping system. The system was managed by a very competent accountant and veteran employee with a knack for keeping impeccable records that no tax auditor would ever have questioned, and only insiders could interpret as connected with wholesale drug traffic.

Like corporate executives, Fitz surrounded himself

with a small circle of qualified experts whose silence could be relied on for any number of reasons, principally because their involvement in his affairs went deep enough to rule out betrayal.

He also felt that educated, middle-class persons were more trustworthy than others. Before hiring them, he checked on their professional ability as well as to see whether they possessed what he called (words indeed curious coming from his lips) a certain standard of ethics. That standard did not disallow engagement in illicit activities, which in fact attracted them to his organization in the first place and without which experience Fitz would not have taken them in, although it did, in his view, inhibit them from turning informer. Fitz differed in that respect from numerous other bosses in the drug trade: a man of taste and education, he abhorred gangster types and studiously avoided them.

Herrick was a valuable aide, especially for hiring new men. Former personnel director of a large corporation, he possessed keen psychological insights developed through study and experience. When forced to resign for embezzlement, he was hired at once by Fitz to do essentially the same kind of work, with a share in the profits that made his previous salary look pitiable. From the start Herrick proved a boon to his new employer. An ace recruiter with an instinctive feel for an applicant's merits or demerits, he could eliminate the potentially dangerous or undesirable ones and put the others to the most efficient use. This applied to jobs all the way up the ladder.

He was a man of authority as well, who attained excellent results by dealing firmly but fairly with the host of hirelings he supervised under Fitz's overall direction. After proving his loyalty, he became Fitz's lieutenant, his adviser at times, even for operations beyond Herrick's competence. He would have been his friend if Fitz had been capable of friendship.

"I assume this Butler warrants the risk."

"As far as I can tell; I'm having him watched, of course. Up to now he's all right. What I like most is that he seems to have good intuition."

"Invaluable asset," Fitz agreed. "What makes you think so?"

"On his own he nosed out and turned down a self-declared addict whom I suspect was a plant from the Narcotics Bureau."

"Not bad for a beginner. . . and he's really hooked? You're sure of it?"

"I've seen the needlemarks, and his manner of approaching me left no doubt: typical state of desperation, though not severe enough yet to dull all inhibitions. I had him take some medical tests; he's still in pretty good condition. I don't think he's increased his dose since he started work a month ago. I expect we'll be able to use him for quite a while."

"Good."

The conversation was taking place at Fitz's luxurious but unostentatious estate in suburban New York. Fitz was in his fifties, a good-looking man, tall and imposing; meticulous about his appearance, he paid an excellent tailor outrageous prices to camouflage his incipient paunch, while his barber managed to create marvelous effects with a few thin strands. Bright-eyed behind slender spectacles, he looked like a board chairman dealing with grave and important matters. In fact that was one side of his personality. He managed a number of highly reputable commercial enterprises in addition to his illegal operations, giving equal time and attention to both. Serving on these administrative councils was extremely remunerative and enabled him to live the kind of life he desired—surrounded by tasteful luxury. His decision to traffic in drugs thus derived more from the lure of adventure than from financial greed.

He had made a success of this business as of many others. From modest, cautious beginnings, he built up an organization whose volume of trade now matched that of older, established competitors. He was proud of his organization, convinced that it could out-perform all others —being more stable, more secure, and possessed of a superior breed of employee. The wise course, he told himself, was to steer clear of underworld connections. He had his own sources of supply, his own exclusive purveyors, his warehouses, his distribution centers, his personal contacts with police and customs officials. His prominent business position would shield him, he hoped, from the prying eyes of the law as well as from those jealous competitors who might learn of his success.

Like any corporate chief worth his salt, he spent a good deal of time studying the machinery he had created with an eye to improving its function and efficiency. Though more inclined to concentrate on general objectives, his broad grasp of which frequently amazed Herrick, he never failed to examine details. For one thing, he kept close tabs on his subordinates through Herrick.

"These pushers shouldn't cause you any problems," he said. "I think you can find as many as you need."

"Just about. But the best aren't out on the streets. When I think I've found one, I try to nab him."

Fitz seemed pleased at this. "Excellent. Don't hesitate to promise a bonus when they deserve it."

"I did just that with Butler when he turned away the agent provocateur."

"I'll always back you up in such cases." And having

31

demonstrated once again that no aspect of the business escaped his attention, Fitz turned to general matters of broader scope. The bulk of his sellers, addicts to whom he paid a minimal wage, gave him no trouble. From time to time one of them might get picked up by the police, but that was nothing to worry about because they had contact only with underlings as ignorant as themselves of the organization's set-up. They rarely saw Herrick, who went by a pseudonym, and didn't know where he lived. In any case, Herrick always managed to whitewash himself in case of trouble. Besides, the police were stepping in less and less, actually at the request of the Narcotics Bureau, which didn't want to scare off big game by pinching the small fry.

The organization employed other types of workers, however. In reviewing them with his boss, Herrick had to admit that their carriers, for example, were not easy to keep in line. The majority were not on drugs and therefore could not be kept under constant surveillance, in the palm of his hand so to speak, like the pushers in the New York district. These carriers, more or less international operators, behaved highly independently. They handled large quantities of drugs and demanded to be paid well for it. Fitz didn't stint on that score; the problem, however, was their behavior—they acted rashly, lived far above their apparent means, spent a lot of time in nightclubs where they drank too much and drew attention. Such evenings occasionally culminated in a raid and the confiscation of merchandise, creating financial losses for the organization much to Fitz's grief and Herrick's anger.

"I can find all the carriers we need among the small fry," said Herrick, "former servicemen, tourists, roving hippies happy to earn some money by concealing a few grams or even hundreds of grams of opium, one or two pounds at most in their luggage. Usually they manage to get it through customs, but it would take an army of them to keep us in supply."

"And I don't think it would be a good policy," Fitz asserted. "Some of our competitors tried it, and we did ourselves for a bit, after some costly raids, but I always felt it was a step backward, a piecemeal solution, if you will. What we need, Herrick, are bold and enterprising operators who can deliver in large quantities."

"Fifty kilos of heroin, for instance," Herrick murmured longingly. . . . "Yes, once upon a time you could find people to do that size job; today, though, it's a dying breed."

"Fifty kilos," echoed Fitz, "yes, I'd like that, but about the future. . ." His voice trailed off and he began to meditate, having stressed the word "future" as if it were charged with radiant promise. Herrick kept silent, knowing that at times Fitz hated prying questions. After a pause, Fitz decided to unveil a small corner of his secret thoughts. Without revealing his plans in detail, he liked to sketch out his general policy (an expression he favored) to close aides, feeling that this gave them a sense of organizational solidarity, kept them alert, interested, on their toes. At that stage he welcomed discussion and sometimes heeded advice if he hadn't already made a decision.

"In the future, Herrick, I think we must give up this policy of small- or medium-sized loads and prepare for fewer and much bigger deliveries instead."

"Bigger than fifty kilos?"

"Bigger even than a hundred. *Much* bigger," Fitz insisted, mysteriously. "This is just between the two of us, but I'm convinced it will happen. Law enforcement will drive us to it, and from our point of view it will be a good thing."

Herrick pursed his lips in surprise and skepticism. "The largest shipments thus far have been between three hundred and four hundred kilos and our competitors didn't get by with it. Remember the 'Sudden Caprice' affair?"

"Yes, I remember, but we'll be smarter."

"It will mean careful advance planning."

"Of course; I didn't expect to start tomorrow. Probably not for two or three years. But give it some thought; we'll talk more about it later on, maybe quite soon, for it involves long-term arrangements on all levels, a complete shift in the whole organization."

Herrick had no further objections. They went on to talk about their carriers: which of them seemed most commendable, clever, reliable, and worth encouraging, and which others ought to be dropped. Then they touched on another category of personnel.

"Right now I'm very concerned about the chemists," said Fitz.

Up till then, the chemists were almost entirely outside Herrick's control for the transformation of morphine into heroin took place in France, beyond his jurisdiction. But Fitz had a plan for reorganizing this side of the business also, and proceeded to describe it to his personnel director.

6

THE EXCHANGE TOOK place rapidly in the men's room of a bar frequented by Butler at odd intervals. Having made certain he was alone with the customer, he drew an open pack of cigarettes from his pocket, slid out one bearing an imperceptible mark, and handed it to the man who grabbed it greedily, cramming some bills into Butler's hand. Butler checked the amount before pocketing it—one hundred dollars. The customer didn't bother to check the goods. Confident that the cigarette contained two doses of heroin inside a thin plastic tube buried among the tobacco shreds, he slipped it into a pack of his own where it blended with the others. It wasn't the first time he had supplied himself in this fashion; Butler, he knew, could be depended on not to skimp on the agreed dose.

He also knew the quality was reliable. The heroin from this seller was always top grade, diluted with no more than an acceptable amount of lactose or bicarbonate, unlike the watered-down products sold by most dealers. Fitz took pride in the quality of his merchandise. He personally determined the percentage of filler, which always had to be added to the drug to insure a satisfactory profit, and forbade any tampering with it along the chain of intermediaries. Herrick enforced his orders. In no time, then, and without advertising, employees of the organization had acquired a reputation for selling a drug containing twelve to fifteen percent pure heroin when others were peddling five or six percent, if not less. Fitz maintained that customer loyalty was a major criterion for business success and always paid off. Experience proved him right.

Simple arithmetic demonstrated that his policy provided the organization with a reasonable profit. At the source, natives in remote lands cultivated poppies and harvested opium for which they received between three hundred and five hundred dollars per ten kilograms. Those ten kilograms, in turn, produced about one kilogram of morphine and roughly 850 grams of pure heroin. With the fair dilution practiced by Fitz, and at the current rate of exchange, the multitude of retailers were paying at least $500,000 for that same quantity, or a thousand times the initial cost. To that, of course, one had to add the high expenses of transport, camouflage, middlemen, bribes, and technical specialists who performed the various transformations. On the whole, however, the operation was proving very lucrative and Fitz felt proud to be handling a product with a superior market rating.

From the start, Butler had no trouble selling his packets. New customers invariably returned for more and usually became steady patrons, like the one tonight.

It hadn't taken him long to realize this, and when he did, it filled him, too, with a sense of pride.

The customer dashed away after pocketing his pack of cigarettes. His addiction was costing him about fifty dollars a day, a relatively heavy dose. In need of a fix for several hours, he barely had time to rush off and inject himself in order to avert a crisis. His latest purchase would take him through tomorrow, relieve his turmoil long enough for him to figure out how to get money for the next dose.

Butler, however, was in no hurry. He washed his hands, smoothed his hair, and ambled out with a wave to the bartender who eyed him indifferently. He breathed deeply, feeling that welcome sense of relaxation that always followed a successful sale, for which he took much of the credit. The idea of concealing the drug in a cigarette was his, for Herrick had left his people free to contrive their own camouflage devices.

Butler had come to realize that inventing hiding places was an amusing way to alleviate the constant boredom. He was actually quite pleased with himself for this last contrivance. It wasn't perfect, of course, and he knew that a thorough search would have disclosed the secret; still, it wasn't bad for a novice. Lately, he was always imagining novel schemes, and during the long idle days, after the syringe had instilled its soothing poison, he spent hours dreaming up better, more reliable hiding places—mental gymnastics of a puerile sort which helped nevertheless to keep him alert.

He left the bar and sauntered off, glancing casually around him. No one was following. The few pedestrians in the dark, deserted street paid no attention to him. He walked away, observed momentarily by the bartender, who, with his nose flattened against the window, seemed interested in his gait.

The bartender was familiar with Butler's activities. Unknown to the latter, he also worked under Herrick, in a higher-level position. He was active only in conjunction with large deliveries worth thousands of dollars made to select clients, and such operations were rather rare, one or two a month at most, at irregular intervals. The drug, in varying disguises, came to him an hour or so before a scheduled transaction; the money was paid over to one of the bar's suppliers.

37

In addition to these occasional sales, he passed on valuable information to Herrick about well-heeled drug users or suspicious persons, as well as his reactions to new salesmen like Butler. His expert eye instantly spotted their assets and liabilities. Like any responsible commercial enterprise, the organization exercised hidden control at every level. It was the barman who had reported favorably on Butler.

Observing him that evening, he noticed that the salesman was more relaxed, his manner more assured, his expression less furtive, his appearance neater, his step firmer. The barman made mental notes of this and resolved to give him a good recommendation.

Butler headed for another part of town, a twenty-minute walk and the scene of his sales debut of the month before. Whenever he returned there, it revived the old nostalgic thrill of his first ordeal. Even now he smiled faintly, recalling how Herrick had left him on his own, armed with a few words of advice and caution. The organization's policy was to let newcomers fend for themselves in carrying out a mission and to drop them if they made too many blunders.

The smile broadened as he remembered that agonizing day before starting work. The double dose òf heroin he took hadn't calmed his racing pulse, and when night came, he had ventured out in search of clients. Gradually, a confused jumble of emotions overcame his apprehension; in part a budding interest in the perilous uncertainties lying ahead, in part a nascent desire to earn the implicit trust Herrick had demonstrated by giving him this touchy assignment.

He had started out by trailing two successive individuals who poked along as if waiting for someone or something. Both times, however, he had decided not to approach them. His own experience of addicts and a single glance at the faces of those two people sufficed to assure him that they were not his kind. He ambled past them and looked elsewhere.

His heart leaped when at last he thought he had spotted the real thing—his excitement building as several signs confirmed his subject to be a potential customer in need of a fix, begging for drug. The man was pacing up and down outside a bar mentioned by Herrick as a likely source of business—repeatedly, he approached the entrance, then recoiled as if afraid to enter. When someone came out the door, the man started toward him, then shrank back as if instinctively warned of his error. For the first time, Butler knew the feverish thrill of a hunter stalking his prey, waiting for hours and finally seeing it approach. After walking past the man in order to look at his eyes, Butler's doubt vanished. Slackening his pace, he turned and flashed the enticing smile of a prostitute trying to hook a customer.

No mistake; the man stopped, fastening an imploring gaze on him, greeting his long-awaited savior. No need for speeches.

"How much do you want to spend?"

"Fifty dollars. That's all I have."

He handed him one of the little packets. The man thrust the money at him and fled. A small deal, but an encouraging start that built up his confidence.

In retrospect, he deplored his lack of caution. His own excitement coupled with the customer's impatience had resulted in an exchange in broad daylight right in the middle of the street. Promising himself to be more careful next time, he began at once to devise a series of rather ingenious operational disguises.

True to his word, he became extremely wary, never trusting a stranger without first examining him thoroughly. This prudent attitude combined with his own good instincts to make him reject the entreaties of an individual who struck him as insincere. The man exhibited all the classic symptoms of an addict in desperate need: tearing eyes, running nose, facial tic, trembling hands, and that imploring look. Too imploring perhaps—having experienced the symptoms firsthand, Butler thought the look exaggerated. He let him talk and was careful not to give himself away, pretending to lend a sympathetic ear to a fellow creature's sufferings. As the man whined on, Butler became convinced he was a fraud. Every now and then his hands ceased to tremble, his features relaxed as if the mask were a strain. Finally he voiced a direct plea, "For pity's sake, can't you tell me where to get some! I'm frantic! I'll pay whatever I have to."

Frowning sternly, Butler proceeded to lecture him on his disgraceful vice, then relented after a while, adopting the solicitous tone of a priest counseling a confessed sinner. In the end, he urged the man to go straight to a drug clinic, mentioning Dr. Edmund's as a place that took in addicts and asked no questions.

The recollection of his self-assured performance in that little comedy brought another smirk of satisfaction to Butler's lips. The scene had taken place in a far corner of the same bar where he had operated tonight. No one could have overheard the conversation, yet the bartender read their gestures out of the corner of his practiced eye. He knew what was going on all the more because he suspected the man of being a narcotics agent. After receiving the bartender's report of the incident, Herrick began to think highly of his new recruit and decided to give him a large bonus which encouraged Butler and helped to convince him he was on the right track.

The agent, on the other hand, was obliged to submit a report of utter failure to his superiors. Stephens was baffled when he read it.

7

HE ENDED HIS night rounds after resupplying several times, having made it a practice to leave his drug supply in a safe place and take with him only the exact number of cigarettes needed for a transaction: five or six at most, but generally one or two for customers of modest means. Oddly enough, he who had once found it impossible to index cards correctly, or add up a column accurately, now had no trouble keeping track in his head of what he had sold, what was left on hand, and how much he had been paid.

Having run out of drug midway through the night, he calculated his receipts at about $4,000. He headed for a bar where Herrick had promised to meet him—well outside Butler's usual business haunts and patronized by a smart crowd without drug connections. Herrick always went to the same one. He and Butler rarely met. The heroin was delivered to Butler by a confederate, the receipts deposited in a sham account. But as the personnel director wished to keep in touch with his employees, he arranged from time to time for a little private chat to discuss their work and thus strengthen the ties binding them to the organization.

Butler always enjoyed these talks. Since the day their paths had chanced to cross, he had become increasingly grateful to Herrick. By assigning him regular work, Herrick had transformed his existence, making it possible for him to earn not only his living but his vital drug ration as well, and the latter in an entertaining fashion. Moreover, Herrick's forthright manner affected him strongly; Butler rarely had encountered such an understanding attitude. On the few occasions when he had run across former classmates, they had been quick to perceive his addiction. The scorn he detected, or thought he detected, stung him deeply and sent him scurrying back into his shell.

Nor had he ever felt at ease with the people in Dr. Edmund's facility, after his second drug cure. From the outset he sensed that the nursing staff, disguised as "companions," couldn't really help him despite their too evident good will. True, they didn't despise him, at least not openly; but they fussed over him constantly, trying to make him feel at home. He suspected that those elaborate demonstrations were carried out in compliance with strict orders. It made him feel inferior, a feeling he detested. After three days he ran off, unable to stand it any longer.

To compound the problem, he had made no friends in drug circles. Paradoxically, he seemed to harbor resentment for other addicts—a feeling which persisted when they became his customers. In fact, he despised them even more when they needed him.

Herrick had been able to put him at ease during their first meeting. He was sympathetic but restrained, cordial yet unaffected, an authority figure who posed no threat and was even likable. Owing to constant exposure earlier in his career to workers up and down the line, office personnel, and all types of people, Fitz's right-hand man had to have acquired broad experience in human relations, a valuable asset in dealing with addicts which he had continued to refine and develop.

He welcomed Butler with a smile as the young salesman joined him in the back room of the bar; he invited him to sit down and to order a drink. Butler's face lit up at the handshake he received; then he noticed that his boss was not his usual serene self. He seemed worried. Butler grew alarmed, fearing that he was in for a reprimand. He was wrong on that score but right in interpreting the concern. Herrick had a problem to resolve.

A personnel problem, unrelated to Butler. Herrick had been running the facts through his head ever since his arrival, lost in meditation, the drink in front of him untouched.

The activities of the Narcotics Bureau were becoming a constant menace to the organization. Though the Bureau had ceased more or less to hunt down pushers, whose arrests merely served to make the bigwigs more wary, its efforts abroad were wreaking havoc on supplies and transport. Worse still, the Bureau had recently carried its attack to clandestine laboratories where the heroin was derived from its morphine base. Still fresh in Herrick's ears was the sound of Fitz bemoaning these new assaults in a recent talk they had had. "The best chemists, mainly French, are now in hiding and unavailable for years to come. We have no competent replacements in France. The qualified people are afraid, and the ones who step forward in hopes of reaping a fortune are bungling amateurs who turn out a third-rate product no one will want to buy. If this continues, addiction may be wiped out because users will refuse to consume such trash. That will mean the end of us. The Narcotics Bureau is counting on this, and I must say they have a point."

The outlook seemed grim indeed, Herrick had to agree. But like a seasoned fighter, Fitz was already preparing to ward off future blows, working out plans to reorganize this sector of the business just as he had intimated that he was doing for the transportation problem. It was all part of an ambitious plan, as Herrick would learn in due time. In the course of the conversation, rapping his fist on the table, Fitz had exclaimed, "We need chemists, Herrick, simple as that! Chemists to turn morphine into heroin. And now this is *your* problem. You must concentrate on this category of personnel which never concerned you till now. Competent chemists, Americans, since the French ones aren't available. Isn't this country the leader in science and technology?"

"Difficult," murmured Herrick uneasily. "I have no connections with scientific circles."

"Make them. . . . And don't forget that I always look far ahead. If you can't find licensed chemists, then train them; take students and turn them into specialists. The situation isn't critical yet and we still have time; one more reason not to be caught napping. I've been thinking about this for years. An organization the size of ours ought to have its own chemists and be free of pressures from abroad. When you've hired a few, then we can consider reorganizing our set-up; send the recruits to France, perhaps, though surveillance there is on the increase; perhaps build laboratories here and import morphine or opium instead of heroin."

"Higher shipping charges," objected Herrick.

"I know. The best solution would be to establish laboratories in opium-producing countries and send our American chemists over to replace the Chinese in Laos and Burma who are equally incapable of turning out a decent product that appeals to our boys and girls. I'm giving it serious thought, and have been for some time. But it's not a plan that can be worked out in a matter of days or even months. The urgent problem right now, Herrick, is for you to find me chemists."

44

Herrick knew from the tone of his voice that Fitz meant business and wouldn't tolerate a failure. He was thinking about the problem when Butler arrived. He tried to forget about it and to concentrate on maintaining his influence over the staff by engaging in these cordial, informal chats. At this late hour the place was nearly empty. Three or four night owls were having one last drink at the bar; the back room was deserted.

"How did it go tonight?"

"I sold everything I had, sir." Butler's habit of calling him "sir" seemed to persist despite friendly remonstrances from Herrick whom it outwardly amused and inwardly flattered.

"Fine. No suspicious persons?"

"None. I dealt only with known, reliable customers."

"Excellent. That makes how much?"

Butler cited the exact figure. Herrick nodded approvingly.

"I'll deposit the money tomorrow."

"Less your commission, of course."

"Thank you, sir."

"Now that I think of it, Butler. . ." As he was bringing the glass to his lips, Herrick suddenly stiffened.

"What is it, sir?"

He didn't answer immediately, setting the glass down again. An idea had just occurred to him. He thought a moment longer before speaking. "I'm very pleased with you, Butler," Herrick declared, sounding faintly paternal. "And how do you feel? Do you like the work? If not, I want you to be sure and tell me so."

The young man flushed with pleasure. He liked compliments of this sort, one of Herrick's prime tools for controlling the staff. Butler protested that he was very happy with what he was doing, his voice ringing with conviction.

Herrick seemed doubtful however, and pursued his train of thought, frowning. "What about drugs? . . . I mean for your personal use?"

In addition to a sales commission, their verbal understanding had stipulated a daily dose of heroin for Butler. The salesman assured him that he considered the product top quality and had no further demands to make. Herrick pressed him. "I'm aware that we put out a good product. But isn't it time to alter our agreement as to quantity? To put it plainly, don't you need to increase your dose? It happens, I know, and I can understand it."

Had Butler been observant, he would have sensed that the strained, apprehensive curiosity behind these questions related to something more than concern for his own person. Herrick leaned forward, staring at him as if afraid to hear his reply. But the young man interpreted this merely as solicitude and answered in a voice trembling with gratitude, "Thank you very much, sir, but our agreement is fine. I don't have to increase my dose."

It was true. Whereas he had found it necessary to raise his intake slightly each week before starting work in the organization, now his need seemed to have leveled off. His daily dose, fairly heavy at that, sufficed to give him peace of mind once the euphoric surge had subsided minutes after withdrawal of the needle. Herrick heaved a sigh of relief and complimented him. "That's fine because addicts on high doses become unable to work for us and we have to drop them. I see you can discipline yourself and I congratulate you. Besides, I thought so all along. You look healthy and your hands have only a slight tremor."

That was also true. Tonight he steered his glass to his lips with a firm hand. Herrick, whom nothing escaped, had noticed it. "Tell me frankly, Butler, selling does indeed require tact and has a certain appeal. But after all, . . . you're a smart fellow, you've been to college, haven't you thought of putting your abilities to better use?"

"You're not thinking of firing me?" Butler protested in alarm.

Herrick eyed him now with the intense interest he occasionally derived from the human side of his relations with Butler. Experience told him the truth: here, now distressed, was a good worker who liked his job and feared dismissal. A searching look convinced him that the addict would do anything to remain in the organization. He hastened to reassure Butler in that faintly paternal tone he employed so effectively. "My dear boy, what are you talking about! I tell you we're very pleased with your work, myself and others. As a matter of fact, I was thinking about promoting you."

"A promotion?"

"A promotion involving not only a raise, which is nothing to sneer at, but also a chance to use your talents. I recall your once telling me that you took some science courses, isn't that so?"

Butler's head drooped contritely. "Yes, I did, but that was ages ago and my grades were terrible. I. . ."

Herrick dismissed his objections. "I know, I know, you told me that. Not everyone can become an eminent scientist. But some of it must have rubbed off on you. . . much more than you think, I'm willing to bet. I know you pretty well by now—you're too modest. Isn't it true that you took some special training in chemistry?"

Butler nodded, unable to comment before Herrick resumed. "Well, this is really a coincidence, Butler, a bit of luck. It just so happens that our organization is in urgent need of chemists."

8

THE PROPOSAL TO assign him to the organization's chemical arm both excited and alarmed Butler's troubled spirit.

On the one hand, he realized that it represented a
promotion, warranted no doubt by his industry, yet un-
foreseen. He also gathered from Herrick's comments that
his employers faced some kind of dilemma and earnestly
wished to serve them in whatever way they asked in order
to repay their generosity. At the same time, however, he felt
unworthy of their attention and expectations. It was probably his own fault to have encouraged Herrick to think well
of him; he should have stressed his unworthiness in their
previous talks. A sense of shame had dissuaded him from
presenting himself in too sorry a light. Now he regretted it
bitterly. The result, nothing short of a crisis on his terms,
was that Herrick now relied on him to do something he
couldn't. He knew absolutely nothing about chemistry
zero. He couldn't remember a single theory and had had no
practice at all, having cut every lab session at school. For
the first time in his life he felt guilty and remorseful for his
squandered schooling.

On the night Herrick made this proposal, Butler lacked
the courage to correct his false impression. The possibility
of disappointing someone intent on helping him better

himself nearly drove him frantic. He responded vaguely, with a stammer, promising to get straight to work, review his notes, collect his textbooks, find out about the latest techniques and do research in whatever specialty they wanted. He needed a short time to see whether he could perform the job. Herrick endorsed this program and wished him luck.

The reference to his school notes was pure fabrication. The notes didn't exist, a handful of scribbled sheets he had burned the day he left school. As for the textbooks, they had long since gone to pay for drugs.

He bought another set. Fired by his ambition to live up to expectations shared by Herrick and the powerful persons above him, Butler geared himself for the fray.

First, he bought a number of useful-looking books on his special topic. They turned out to be beyond his grasp. He realized that to comprehend them he would have to build a basic knowledge of chemistry. So he bought other textbooks more general in scope. Before long his whole salary was spent and he had nothing to eat. This was no great hardship, however, for his dependable daily drug ration acted as a substitute for food. After assembling a fairly extensive library, he settled down to study during the day and on those nights when he was not hanging around shabby bars on the lookout for customers.

But books were not enough. He soon perceived, with discouragement verging on despair, that his sluggish brain, dulled by years of inactivity, refused to obey his budding will. Or was it the drug in his system that made it impossible to concentrate on a passage and memorize the simplest formula? When this occurred to him, he found the courage to renounce his daily dose. The results were even worse.

49

After two days of withdrawal, he felt so sick that he feared further abstinence might immobilize him completely. He tried doubling the dose with no noticeable improvement in his mental faculties. Common sense made him revert to his normal intake, and he looked for some other way to achieve his purpose.

Alone, he would never make it, he kept telling himself during those endless, frustrating hours. I need help, he thought. Not knowing where to find it, he was about to drag himself defeated before Herrick when a stroke of luck befell him. A face emerged from the blurred memories of his school years: he recalled the graceless profile of Bridget, several years his senior, a graduate chemistry student assisting in the laboratory while he was an undergraduate.

Her face flashed through his mind as he struggled vainly to untangle the barbaric gibberish of formulas. With her drooping shoulders, the intensely bookish set of her jaw, her watery gaze, she had been one of the top students at school. At the time he knew her, she was somewhere between student and teacher, ill at ease among both. Her unattractive looks merely added to her isolation.

This undoubtedly had brought them together. She was the only person with whom he attempted to strike up the semblance of a friendship. But even that didn't get very far, for she spent all her time studying while he frittered his away.

He hadn't thought of her for years. As her face loomed before his eyes, out of a jumble of chemical symbols, it occurred to him that she might be the helpmate he so desperately needed. Hadn't she once offered to tutor him? He had backed off after one session and given up, but now the situation was totally different.

What had become of her? A frantic search uncovered her telephone number in an old address book and he resolved to give it a try, expecting to reach some other party.

A familiar voice answered; he felt immense relief, convinced that help was finally at hand. Excitement lent a note of rapture to his otherwise trite speech. The thrill seemed to strike an echo on the other end. Of course she remembered him! Of course she wanted to see him again! They met on the appointed day, prompted by different motives but the same enthusiasm.

He recognized her instantly; she hadn't changed or improved much. He was pleased to see her step forward eagerly to meet his advance, hand outstretched, visibly happy to rediscover an old friend.

They lunched in a plain little restaurant. After they had exchanged civilities, and without knowing how to say what he wanted, he insisted on hearing what she had been doing since they lost touch. She warmed to this solicitude and began her tale, broken by pauses during which his eyes never left her.

The gist of it was simple. Feeling that she was getting nowhere, she had quit college to look for employment in the chemical industry, but lacking both contacts and the art of exploiting her superior education, obtained only mediocre job offers. Out of discouragement, she finally accepted an inferior position in a pharmacological laboratory. She had been there for two years and was fairly content, but couldn't get too excited about the routine work. Having moved up the ladder by degrees, she was now in charge of a major department and felt financially secure. "Which is something, after all," she sighed, wistfully.

He hastened to agree, and in a series of artful questions designed to reveal only his intense interest in her, managed to worm out information about this department.

"We do a number of things, too many to enumerate. We test pharmaceuticals and also various drugs. For instance, one of my sections is doing research on possible substitutes for dangerous poisons like heroin."

Butler's ears perked up; by now he was more or less confident that Bridget would save him.

"Another section is in touch with the Narcotics Bureau, which sometimes has us run analyses."

With great difficulty he repressed a shudder. Her contact with an organ which dealers, even on his humble level, feared more than the police, seemed to threaten his plan. Her next words, however, reassured him. Her contact with the Bureau was purely technical, involving analysis and identification of drugs seized by narcotics agents in periodic raids: mainly heroin, backbone of the drug traffic. Also examination of products uncovered in clandestine laboratories and other similar investigations.

These facts served merely to confirm his initial, instinctive response: she was an angle in disguise. No one came better equipped than she to provide the help he needed, to initiate him into the mysteries of that delicate transformation of morphine into heroin, so crucial to the organization of which he had begun to consider himself a full-fledged member. With luck, maybe he could even ferret out some information on the Bureau that would be useful to his superiors.

What should be his first step? He was thinking about this, not realizing that she had stopped talking and was watching him intently.

"You know all about me," she said at last, "but what have *you* been doing since college?"

For a moment he said nothing, feigning far more embarrassment than he really felt; then, as if reaching a decision, he poured out an abject confession. "Nothing good, which shouldn't come as a surprise after what you know of me already. A stint in the army, and now I'm jobless, nearly t the end of my rope, without a single degree and no skill o help me earn a living." After pausing for effect, he coninued, "If you only knew how much I admire your passion or study, your perseverance. My only goal today is to get a ob, any kind of job. But, I never will. Time lost, the years f my youth wasted an idleness, all that is irreparable."

"You must never say or believe that!" she protested vehemently. "Your feeling of regret in itself is encouraging. Nothing is irreparable."

"Do you really think so?" The glow of hope burning in his eyes was not part of the comedy he was acting out. "Do you really think so? That's what I sometimes tell myself. But alone as I am at the moment, I'd never have the courage and determination to struggle against the current."

"You can always row against the current," she declared matter-of-factly. "All it takes is the right person handling the oars."

Part Two

Part

Two

1

BRIDGET CLEARED HER throat and continued dictating the lecture notes she had written for Butler. "Alkaloids. History and definition. Knowledge of alkaloids, glucosides, and other constituents of vegetable origin dates back to 1803 when Charles Derosne succeeded in deriving a syrupy extract from opium which he crystallized, after diluting it in water and purifying it. Thus, he prepared the first alkaloid, probably relatively impure narcotine. By adding soda to this product, he obtained a different substance—presumably, morphine. . . ."

She paused on a sign from Butler who had fallen behind. He was trying to fathom the meaning of each word before writing it down, so the work progressed slowly. She resumed when he had caught up with her.

"Today, despite our still imperfect knowledge of alkaloids, we can safely say that they are relatively complex substances with basic properties, found in their natural state in plants, and which exert marked physiological effects. Several alkaloids are liquid and contain only three elements: carbon, hydrogen, and nitrogen, but the majority also contain oxygen and appear in the form of colorless crystalline solids. Example: opium contains at least twenty-five different alkaloids, the most important of which is morphine, $C_{17}H_{19}O_3N$. . . ."

Seated opposite Bridget, he was taking elaborate notes in a spiral binder already three-quarters filled. He had been doing this several times a week now for nearly six months.

". . . Morphine crystallizes into colorless prisms containing one molecule of water, which it gives up at 212° F. The anhydrous alkaloid dissolves at 489° F. and has a rotation in methyl alcohol of. . ."

She wasn't leaving a thing out! At least they were getting to the part that really interested him. Not quite yet, but it wouldn't be long.

What patience he had mustered just to get that far! Several months earlier, at the close of their first meeting when she had found him so upset, she herself had made the very suggestion he couldn't bring himself to voice: "Listen, people often think they haven't learned a thing or have forgotten it all, but I'm sure you must have retained certain fundamentals."

Herrick had said the same thing. Despite Butler's manifest deception, he so wanted it to be true that he began to believe it himself.

"If you regret the past and if you really want to resume your studies. . ."

"I do, I do, but. . ."

"Then, I'd like to help you. I did a little teaching once at school and since then I've tutored students on and off, with pretty good results."

"Would you do that?"

"Gladly. And if, as I hope, you work very hard and acquire a solid grasp of the subject, you can earn a certificate of study equivalent to a college degree which will be very valuable. Then maybe I can find a job for you in the laboratory where I work. They think highly of me."

It wasn't exactly an idyllic situation, but the program she outlined seemed tempting. He accepted gratefully and with enthusiasm. "How long will it take, do you think?"

"That depends mainly on you. A year or two perhaps, if you work steadily."

"A year or two! That's far too long. I think I can make better progress. I promise you I'll become a grind; I'll give up my sleep."

"We'll see. Don't make too many rash promises. It will be hard in the beginning."

At Butler's insistence, the lectures began the very next day in the small apartment she had once shared with a girlfriend until she could afford to occupy it alone.

She was right: it was terribly hard at first, but he clung doggedly to this anchor and managed to overcome his innate apathy in a surge of intellectual effort that no one would have thought him capable of mobilizing. The effort was all the more painful since Bridget, who had no inkling that his interest lay in one narrow, special channel, set out, as promised, to give him a sound education in chemistry, not just a smattering, hoping it would lead to a job later on. From the very first lesson, she warmed to the challenge, seeking to expand the already ambitious program she had designed for him with pedagogical thoroughness—an undertaking which demanded considerable preparation from her as well. A charitable soul, she suffered the imprisoning loneliness of her timidity and inhibitions, and thus far had never found an outlet for her need to serve. Confused and upset when first she saw him, Butler provided this outlet. Besides, she was visibly drawn to this bewildered, overgrown child.

He was ready to send her packing after hearing her

outline the course of study, which he thought inhuman
—beginning with the general laws of chemistry, progressing to mineral chemistry, then exploring the monstrous
field of organic chemistry before reaching the specialized
work of her own laboratory, principally the transformation
of morphine into heroin. He yielded in the end, but only
after a violent inner struggle.

She was his last hope; he had to bend to her will. He
resigned himself to her study program; they started with
the basic laws governing the behavior of matter, from pri-
mary elements to the most complex compounds. He was
also forced to memorize formulas, the very sight of which
made him shudder.

After several weeks of excruciating mental torture, he
began to notice the discipline became less and less painful.
The day finally arrived when, convinced that what he was
learning would be useful for the job he was expected to
perform, he could sit down to work without a sense of loathing. From that point on, he plugged away with renewed
vigor and inside of six months had covered nearly the entire
course.

". . . Morphine is most commonly used for medical purposes in the form of a sulfate, represented by the
formula. . ."

At last his efforts were to be rewarded. Having guided
him through the maze of analyses and syntheses for a host
of elements, she was finally taking up the study of alkaloids:
today, morphine, the focus of all his thinking. He smiled at
her and continued taking notes.

The lessons were still held in Bridget's apartment. He
explained that it would have embarrassed him to invite her

to his shabby place. After one or two lectures, they became lovers. She had made the first move; on his part, he saw no reason to alter their relationship but feared his refusal might hurt her feelings and discourage her from helping him all she could.

In any event, love-making was never allowed to interfere with the study schedule. Both of them saw to that; he, because she didn't really attract him and every moment was precious; she, because devoting much time to sexual frolic would have given her a guilty sense of professional laxity. She was very proud of her pupil's rapid strides. Having once aspired to be a college professor, she often regretted having cut short her studies in order to earn a living. The task she had assumed bore a tinge of revenge; she performed it with priestly dedication and ardor.

Smiling back at him, she stopped dictating and resumed a conversational tone. "Morphine produces heroin, a derivative much talked about in recent years—a highly pernicious drug of great interest to the Bureau of Narcotics for which my lab does occasional work. Nine-tenths of the samples they send us for testing have a heroin base, refined by crude methods and equipment, yet with amazing success at times. It's called diacetylmorphine. The extraction process is simple in theory but troublesome in practice, and the purity of the final product can vary greatly according to the chemist's skill. . . . That will be tomorrow's lesson, darling."

She shut the notebook containing the lectures she composed, sometimes late at night, in order to cover a subject thoroughly and make it easier for him to understand. He felt like cursing her and had to restrain a sneer. Though dying to learn all about this topic at once, he was afraid to press her and risk arousing her suspicions. For he had

61

never told her of his membership in the society of addicts and was sure she hadn't guessed it. Reluctantly, he stood up and took her in his arms.

"Darling, I don't know what I'd do without you," he said, holding her close.

Smiling, she abandoned herself to his embrace on the studio couch, blissfully unaware that instead of making love that night he would by far have preferred to attain the goal he had dreamed of all these months, the one and only ambition inspiring him with the will to pursue this tedious task.

2

STEPHENS WAS READING a voluminous report when one of his assistants asked to see him. Hired as an ordinary office agent, Allen had won praise from his superiors for capable, intuitive handling of several touchy matters. Stephens, who also demanded high qualifications of his employees and spent a good deal of time selecting them, had advanced him rapidly, despite his youth and the frowns of senior staffers, to the rank of a chief aide.

He pointed to a chair opposite his desk, pushing aside a pile of statistical reports.

"I'm listening, Allen. Is it important? Are you on the trail of the King of Drugs?"

"No, sir, something else is bothering me and I thought you ought to be informed. It's about Butler."

"You mean the ex-G.I. I told you to keep under surveillance?"

"Yes. He hasn't been arrested, but I'm almost certain he's involved in selling drugs."

"He wouldn't be the first, would he?"

"It also appears that he meets with Herrick now and then."

"That's fine, but do we have anything new and solid on Herrick?"

"Only what you already know, sir. I've had his apartment searched several times by expert housebreakers. They couldn't find a trace of drugs."

"That doesn't surprise me. He's a clever fellow, too important to take such risks, unless our suspicions are completely unfounded. So? You didn't ask to see me about something I already know."

"A new development in Butler's contacts, sir. Until recently, like a good many addicts, he led a lonely life. Well, for the past month he's been seeing a girlfriend regularly."

Knowing his aide to be a sober-minded fellow, Stephens looked him squarely in the eye. "That's not unusual, you realize. I can only assume, since you bring it up, that it's no ordinary affair—that he hasn't latched onto a prostitute the way many addicts do."

"Hardly a prostitute, sir; she's a very respectable girl with a responsible job in a good firm. The reason I mention it is because I think you already know her. A chemist."

"Chemist?"

"She runs a department in the pharmacological laboratory we use occasionally to do our testing. Her name is Dodge, Bridget Dodge."

Stephens whistled softly in surprise. "Bridget Dodge! Of course I know her. I've dealt with her often. She's always seemed intelligent and competent. Now you think. . ."

"Only what I've told you, sir. She and Butler have been seeing each other several times a week. He stays at her place for hours, sometimes overnight. That's all."

"That's all? Isn't it enough? An addict presumably in touch with drug peddlers getting cozy with the manager of a. . . good Lord, Allen, I'm glad you told me!"

"The relationship may be nothing special at all," Allen added hastily. "I've checked it out; they were in school

64

ogether, chemistry majors as a matter of fact. It seems
natural that they became friends. Anyway, I thought I ought
to mention it, because of her job."

"I'm very glad you did. A respectable girl, to all
appearances. . . we'll have to keep an eye on her, too."

"I've been doing just that for the past few weeks. I put
off speaking to you until my report was ready."

"And?"

"Negative results. I'm convinced she's all right and has
no link with the drug trade. Nothing suspicious except her
relations with Butler."

"Isn't she on drugs?"

"I would have thought so; she has ample opportunity at
work. But there's no evidence of it. Her performance on the
job is just as efficient as ever and she doesn't behave like an
addict."

"So what's your conclusion?"

"They're good friends, I suppose; maybe she's even in
love with him, but in either case she ought to know the risks
involved in such an association."

"I'll have to warn her. But what in the devil does she
see in him, Allen? I've never met the fellow, yet from
Edmund's story he hardly sounds like a Don Juan: he's
fainthearted, lazy, withdrawn, unmanly; she's bookish,
energetic. . ."

"And not overly endowed with sex appeal. I've seen
her a few times and that's how she struck me. I'm not passing judgment on her, but I'd guess she hasn't had men
swooning at her feet."

"I suppose you're right. It will only make it harder to
convince her. Anyway, I'll do my best."

3

BEFORE GOING OVER to the pharmacological laboratory Stephens dropped in on Dr. Edmund to consult him about another matter. After settling it, they naturally turned to the subject of Butler, and Stephens confided to the psychiatrist his alarm at the former serviceman's current affair, of course without naming the woman involved. He was going to alert her, he said. Edmund tried to discourage him.

"It's probably the best thing that can happen to him, Stephens. As I've often told you, a woman can be the architect of a lasting cure if she goes about it properly... You say she's principled and stable? Maybe she'll have sufficient influence on him to straighten him out. If I were you, I wouldn't interfere."

"It's easy for you to talk, Doctor. My job is not to straighten him out."

Stephens ultimately decided to disregard this excellent medical advice. No narcotics agent could afford to allow a relationship to develop between someone like Butler and a woman with access to confidential information about the drug traffic. Leaving the doctor's office, he went to the laboratory, feeling a certain sense of guilt.

Bridget was not working. She couldn't bring herself to do it

nd, instead, was reading over and over a shocking letter
eceived that morning. She had barely found the strength to
lrag herself to the office. Her tense features conveyed a
nixture of sorrow and spite. When her secretary announced
a visitor, she rebuked her sharply.

"Can't you see I'm busy? I told you I didn't want to be
listurbed."

"He says he has an appointment, Miss Dodge; it's Mr.
Stephens."

Recalling that he had telephoned the day before, she
growled instructions to have him shown in, tossing the let-
er angrily into a desk drawer.

The conversation got off to an awkward start. Stephens
felt increasingly ill at ease over his part in the affair and the
discomfort grew worse when he saw that she resented his
interference. She bristled at his first clumsy allusion to the
company she was keeping.

"As I understand it, because I do occasional testing for
your agency, you've decided to poke your nose into my
private life?"

"It's not that, really. I simply wanted to alert you, to
spare you a rude awakening."

"Do I owe you some sort of explanation for entertain-
ng a man in my apartment?"

"Listen, Bridget, you're perfectly free to entertain men
in your apartment whenever you like, dozens of them, if it
suits you; the Narcotics Bureau doesn't give a hoot. It so
happens that the man in question has come to our attention,
not because he visits you, but for a very serious reason.
Because I respect you I feel I must warn you about his real
personality."

"What do you mean?"

"First of all, that Butler uses drugs, not just casual-

67

ly, but steadily, and has been for years; he is probably an incurable addict. That's only the first point. Futhermore. . ."

He paused, his detective's instinct prompting him to observe the effect produced by this disclosure. She never winced and kept looking him straight in the eye.

"I suppose then," she said contemptuously, "that you suspect me of furnishing him with narcotics from the laboratory shelves.'

"I don't suspect any such thing. I know you and I know that he has other sources of supply."

Shrugging her shoulders, she dropped her eyes and spoke in less hostile tones. "I knew it."

"You knew it?"

"The first time we made love. I doubt that this is news to you since you were having me watched. I realized it the moment I saw the needlemarks on his arms, on his thighs, on his stomach, all over his body. I never let on that I had discovered his secret, hoping that. . ."

"That what?"

"That he would be cured with. . . with my help," she added, her voice barely audible.

"I understand," said Stephens, visibly moved.

"Don't you see?" she burst out, "I was trying to lift him out of his rut, to free him from his addiction. I was hoping to restore him to a normal life through affection. And I'm sure I would have succeeded; we were making such progress. He continued taking drugs, but his attitude and behavior were no longer those of an addict. Don't you believe me? I know it's true, from my own experience. You call him a hopeless addict? Come now, when was any hopeless addict capable of working?. . . working like a slave for months, I can assure you. I sensed that he was really determined to change his life, and he almost did, thanks to me."

68

Recalling Dr. Edmund's recommendation, Stephens felt more and more flustered. His interference now appeared to be a blunder threatening to disrupt a miraculous cure. Apparently that was her opinion as well, for she spoke of Butler in the past tense, as if their relationship were doomed. He had no chance to ask what kind of work Bridget meant. A question from her reminded him that her lover was under suspicion on more than one count.

"You said this was just the first point?"

"Yes, the second is more serious. Like many addicts, he seems to have fallen in with a gang of dealers and has done a brisk little trade in heroin lately, probably for those gangsters."

He noted that this really seemed to affect her. Undoubtedly, she hadn't known this side of her lover.

"This is my main reason for wanting to alert you."

"Thanks."

She remained silent, brooding. This last disclosure obviously took her by surprise. When she spoke again, her voice was heavy with sarcasm.

"I gather that in view of my job here, the Narcotics Bureau would like to see me break up with him, right?"

"That decision is yours to make."

"Or maybe you'd prefer to have me worm information out of him like one of your spies?"

Stephens flushed. As a matter of fact, the idea had just flitted through his head. Like most conscientious detectives, he grabbed at every source of intelligence. He assured her that no such proposal had ever occurred to him.

"In any case, I'm sorry I can't oblige you," she exclaimed, her voice laden with pained irony. "Do you know why?"

"As I say, you're free to act as you wish."

"You don't get it at all! He's ditched me!" she shouted.

"I'll never see him again; we're ending this compromising affair! But he's the one who's throwing me over! Now are you satisfied?"

Concealing his surprise and embarrassment at this angry, tasteless outburst, Stephens muttered some polite excuse.

"Just as you came in, I was rereading his letter telling me it's all over. Don't you believe me? Here, read it yourself. God forbid I should have secrets from the Narcotics Bureau!"

He could see that she was terribly distraught. She shoved the paper at him so insistently that he finally took it. After a rapid glance at the contents, he read it more carefully and a particular passage caught his eye.

It was indeed a "Dear John" letter, awkward and extremely banal. Nowhere in it did he sense the passion she expressed. With cliché-ridden politeness, Butler thanked her for "her many kindnesses" as well as "the lessons she had patiently given him for which he would be eternally grateful because they would help to make him a new man". This sentence had caught Stephens's eye; it reminded him of something she had said a few minutes before.

The letter ended with a farewell as trite as the rest of the message. "Circumstances independent of his will" obliged him "to his great regret" to part from her. He assured her of his undying love and begged her not to try to see him again. In fact he was leaving the United States, he said, and didn't expect to return for years, if ever.

Stephens handed back the letter, having all but memorized it. Apologizing once more for having upset her, he asked casually, just before leaving:

"What in the devil does he mean by the lessons you're supposed to have given him? Weren't you just talking about his working like a slave?"

She told him the whole story—how, sensing his guilt and remorse over his wasted youth, she had taken pity on him, set herself the task of teaching him, developing his appreciation for learning, and encouraging him to think in terms of an eventual career in chemistry.

"Chemistry?"

"Certainly. It wasn't new to him, besides being the only subject I was competent to teach; later on, maybe I could have found him a job in my laboratory."

It took Stephens a moment to digest the implications of this innocent statement. When he did, he wondered in dismay whether it wasn't some freakish trick of his imagination.

"If I understand you correctly, you're saying that you introduced him to the chemistry of narcotics, that you taught him all the tricks of the trade you practice in your laboratory."

"Among other things. Many other things."

"And you knew he was on drugs!"

"In that respect, I felt he stood to gain by my exposing him to the whole drug picture—stressing its noxious effects and its toxic nature. Complete information can only help such unfortunate persons. Pastry cooks never eat pastry."

"Pastry cooks never eat pastry," Stephens repeated, numbly. "And now, thanks to you, he is in a position to. . ."

He left his sentence dangling, horrified by the image taking shape in his mind. At this point, Bridget burst out with a display of passionate rebellion.

"And I succeeded!" she shouted, "it was all my doing; alone, he never would have made it. And though he's thrown me over, I don't regret a thing. I know he didn't work like a slave for nothing and that some day he'll reap his reward. Then, maybe he'll appreciate what I did for him. . . out of love."

71

"Some day he'll reap his reward," Stephens repeated once more, feeling the rage mounting within him, barely able to contain his urge to throttle her.

Taking hold of himself, he realized suddenly that it was a waste of breath to try to explain his apprehensions. She was captive to her own private, obliquely-worded, fantasies.

"I alone had the capacity to change him," she declared proudly. "You call him an incurable addict? That's a joke. I know him better than you do, despite all your informers. I tell you he worked like a slave, to pry himself out of a rut, to—oh, I see it now, you've opened my eyes—escape the depraved atmosphere threatening to engulf him."

And as Stephens shrugged his shoulders in exasperation, she burst into a flood of tears:

"At least let me believe that he struggled partly for love of me!"

4

THE LABORATORY WAS installed on a ranch in Indiana run by a half-Indian couple. The surrounding range provided sparse grazing for a small herd. The couple lived in virtual isolation, their nearest neighbors miles away and unwilling to associate with half-breeds. Fitz had bought this ranch-land years before, without his name appearing on the deed, thinking that such a retreat might come in handy one day. Herrick lodged the two half-castes there, employed them on and off and found them completely loyal. They managed the ranch badly, and when raising livestock no longer earned them a living, he kept them supplied with liquor, their sole necessity. As a result, they proved utterly discreet, blind and deaf to whatever happened to go on at the ranch.

Having decided to end his dependence on French laboratories and set up his own heroin manufacturing, Fitz selected this as a suitable, temporary site while planning ahead for the future. It was to serve as a prototype, as well as a yardstick for measuring the new chemist's talents.

Delivered secretly by private plane, Butler began his new job. He led a monastic life, surrounded by flat, monotonous plains, seeing no one but the caretakers and them only at mealtime. But feverish zeal for his work kept him from feeling lonely. Having set up Spartan living quarters for himself at the rear of the shed housing the laboratory, he rarely ventured outside the building.

He had gone straight to work upon arrival, after reading over the chapter dictated by Bridget on the manufacture of heroin, or chlorhydrate of diacetylmorphine, from its morphine base. Theoretically, the conversion was simple, far simpler than for many other chemical substances he had learned to analyze and synthesize in the course of all those lectures. He understood both the scientific process and the functions of the various reactions that occurred. In fact, his understanding was so thorough that he would have been capable of lecturing his own students in turn.

The application raised no difficulties either, except in matters of detail. It consisted of heating a mixture of morphine and acetic anhydride at 185° F. for several hours in a water bath. This produced the impure heroin in solution. Then a series of refining processes were necessary, in the course of which, the heroin, in the form of a crystalline precipitate, was supposed to emerge in progressively concentrated form. That was the most delicate stage of the operation, and Butler, in despair, perceived that his results were still imperfect.

When Herrick visited him during a trip to Indiana, Butler confessed sheepishly:

"Purity of final product: only sixty percent. I feel terrible about it, sir."

It was true; Butler looked crushed, like a conscientious worker obliged to admit a serious error. Herrick consoled him with a friendly pat on the shoulder.

"Sixty percent isn't so bad, my boy. You're a newcomer to the trade and many professionals don't do much better. Of course certain underground chemists in France do get superior results, but. . ."

74

This Butler knew. Chemists in licensed laboratories, with a string of degrees and the finest equipment available, still couldn't manage to extract as pure a product as certain unlicensed experimenters operating with crude instruments. This was common knowledge among drug users, dealers, and the Narcotics Bureau. Bridget had commented on this anomaly with pointed sarcasm:

"In running a test using the same basic elements as one of those little crooks, I myself could do no better than sixty-five percent, whereas he produced eighty percent regularly with nothing more elaborate than a set of kitchen tools. The all-time expert," she added ruefully, "was Cesari."

Cesari was a Corsican whose name, in the drug world, became as famous as Napoleon's. Without formal training in any discipline, chemistry least of all, he learned from an individual still more illiterate than himself—a professional cook, apparently, who transmitted to him his magic touch. Cesari was able to turn out a steady ninety-five percent in his illicit workshop somewhere in the vicinity of Marseilles. After his arrest, no professional or amateur ever matched that record.

Bridget had also mentioned that in the line of vocational curiosity she occasionally experimented to try to improve her own results. She might have succeeded, she felt, but for the fact that success depended on lengthy trial-and-error testing which she never had time to complete. In passing, she had indicated to Butler the critical points requiring special care and attention. None of these details was lost on him.

"Of course," Herrick went on, "they've done wonders in France, especially Cesari. Too bad there'll never be another artist to rival him," he sighed. "Anyway, sixty percent is still an improvement over what we get from certain

Chinese makers in the Far East when they try their hand at extraction. We take the percentage into account in diluting it afterwards."

Herrick emphasized the advantages of producing a more concentrated drug: it took up less space, cost less to transport, and was easier to conceal, as well as possessing a number of other positive factors. Actually, the organization was very pleased with Butler's results, which were average, and with his services. He, on the other hand, dissatisfied with his own performance and thinking he detected a hint of reproach in Herrick's remarks, hastened to present a plan he had been ruminating over for some time.

"I'll do my utmost to improve the results, sir, but it calls for further experiments in another vein. Now. . ."

"Experiment all you like, my boy, I'll be the last to stop you. I'm delighted to find you in such a constructive frame of mind."

"Now I have a request to make."

"What's that? Don't you have everything you need here?"

"The equipment is fine and I have plenty of ingredients, but I'd like to conduct some experiments in addition to my normal output for the market, and try to improve the product. This will mean using a small quantity of the morphine base—a very small proportion of it—and of the other ingredients as well. I ought to warn you that the resulting product, in the beginning at least, may not be fit for consumption and therefore a dead loss."

Herrick stared at him with intense fascination. The professional pride this man occasionally displayed was so rare in the trade as to appear utterly astounding.

"I think I understand. You want to do thorough, systematic research, the kind that goes on in large scientific laboratories."

"That's exactly it, sir. I'd like to rediscover Cesari's formula," Butler announced in fervent tones.

Unearth Cesari's magic recipe! Become a drug world celebrity! Present this token of gratitude to his employers! These aspirations had flitted through his head when Bridget had first told him of the Corsican's feats, and eventually they had become rooted there once he ascertained his results to be no better or worse than the work of professional chemists. Now they haunted him day and night, inspiring feverish dreams mingled with narcotic hallucinations.

He had already experimented with varying the heating period and modifying the ratio of ingredients, but in the daily extraction process he scrupulously avoided departing more then a hair's breadth from the classic formula for fear of wasting the product. In order to make progress, he would have to do objective research with samples set aside for that purpose and not worry about spoiling them—to proceed as in all serious experimental laboratories. Bearing in mind the pivotal points stressed by Bridget, he had conceived a plan which he was prepared to implement upon proper authorization.

Herrick remained stunned, unsure what to say. Was it a rational proposal or an extravagant folly, induced perhaps by narcotic euphoria? Someone else would have rejected it out of hand, but his former experience in industry prompted him to consider the matter seriously. He knew that pure research often pays off in the long run, even if the initial outlay is costly and promises no immediate return. He continued to think about it, undecided.

"There's no good reason why we in this country can't work as effectively as an ignorant Frenchman," Butler asserted.

This chauvinistic approach failed to win Herrick's support; he wanted to hear more substantial arguments.

"What percentage of morphine would be sacrificed for your experiments?" he asked at last. "That is the central issue, the other ingredients don't count."

"Not over one percent."

Herrick made a rapid mental calculation. Butler's laboratory turned out approximately twenty-five kilograms of heroin weekly at sixty percent; the proposal entailed giving up one kilogram per month. Costly. Counting the usual dilutions, the loss in sales would run high, around $300,000, he estimated; a maximum, however, for some of it still could be used, Butler insisted. On the other hand, if this clever fellow succeeded in measurably improving the quality, their profits, after two or three months, would shoot up accordingly. That was the principle guiding all basic research.

The spirit of progress won. He concluded finally that the risk was worth taking. Armed with decision-making authority from Fitz, Herrick gave his consent, confident that Fitz in turn would approve.

And he did. With his comprehensive, even visionary, view of business matters, Fitz could hardly reject the proposal. When Herrick returned from his inspection tour and told him about it several days later, Fitz's response was altogether enthusiastic.

"You know, Herrick, I'm very pleased with that fellow. He's just the kind I like. You showed excellent judgment in hiring him and then urging him to better himself. I think we can trust him now."

"I do, too."

The trust had not always been there. Butler's affair with Bridget had inevitably aroused Herrick's suspicions when he learned of it through his intelligence network, nearly as efficient as that of the Narcotics Bureau. Although the girl was rarely in contact with the Bureau, the mere existence of this vague connection with the organization's worst emeny sufficed to alarm him. With the consent of Fitz, who felt as nervous about it as he, Herrick had doubled surveillance of the veteran. His suspicions vanished, however, the day Butler remarked ingenuously that he had discovered in Bridget a benign teacher supremely qualified to help him develop the special chemical expertise he desired.

"Do you think he could ever get to. . . say ninety percent?" Fitz wondered.

"I hope so. His target is even higher."

"It would be particularly interesting in terms of the long-range developments I have in mind. I'd like you to do all you can for him; give him whatever he wants, regardless of the expense."

"I've done so and he's already hard at work. . . . Fitz, that fellow really mystifies me. I've never seen a heroin addict able to apply himself so diligently. Generally, they're limp."

"Are you positive he's an addict?"

"No question of it. I've had him watched—the evidence is all there. He's on a pretty large dose, too. But it seems to have spared his will power, left him fiercely determined to achieve his goal."

"What goal?"

"To match Cesari's record: ninety-five percent."

Fitz whistled softly. "If he could get anywhere near it, life would be infinitely simpler for us."

"That's all he's interested in now. Never takes a day off."

"Don't let him ruin his health, for heaven's sake," Fitz warned, suddenly alarmed by a new concern.

One of the clauses in Butler's unwritten contract, a standard stipulation for all chemists involved in heroin ex-

traction, was a fifteen-day work month intended to protec
him from prolonged handling of the ingredients. Before
giving his consent, Herrick had raised the objection tha
these experiments would waste time and eventually de
crease the laboratory's output. Butler had vowed, however
not to take a single moment from production for the sake o
research, which would claim only his spare time.

"On that basis, I agree. But don't overwork yoursel
my dear fellow," Herrick concluded, anticipating Fitz'
concern. "Your health is too precious to us."

5

HERRICK STAYED ONLY two days on the ranch in Indiana but saw enough to go away satisfied. Each week, like clockwork, the laboratory turned out its twenty-five kilograms of heroin. Deliveries were flown to the New York region and fresh supplies of morphine brought in by a private plane which landed at night on a barren, deserted strip of pasture. The caretaker couple stumbled about in an alcoholic stupor. The chemist was making progress. Only the livestock suffered, but Herrick didn't care.

As soon as Herrick left, Butler went straight to his cubbyhole at the back of the shed. Once again he read over Bridget's lecture on the extraction of heroin, concentrating on the notes he had accumulated gradually from her chance remarks about potential improvements of the traditional procedure.

He slammed the notebook shut; it had nothing more to teach him. The answer lay not in formulas but in a certain empirical touch—a precise combination of ingredients, the audacious introduction of one or another catalyst—a set of procedures not unlike the methods developed by certain renowned chefs after years of experimentation and countless curdled sauces. Unwritten recipes were occasionally transmitted to the next generation by demonstration, but were often lost forever when the master lacked the time to train disciples, as in Cesari's case.

Butler decided to reorder his schedule to accommodate his ambitious project. By going without sleep, he completed his monthly quota inside a few days, leaving the rest of the month free for research.

Once his quota was fulfilled, he could relax, and as he sat at the rickety old table in the dilapidated cubicle which served as both sleeping and study quarters, he experienced an inner glow, more intense than he had ever known, made exhilarating by the drug he had just injected.

It felt as if he were leaping over several levels of some confused hierarchy at a single bound. Until then, disciplined study and the mechanical application of everything he had learned had interested him mildly and given him the satisfaction of conquering his apathy—considerable rewards at that—but today he felt elevated to a higher state. Forced to rely entirely on his own resources, to excite them to the highest degree in order to execute a bold plan defying even the experts, to erect his own framework for the task ahead, to break all the rules, to grope in darkness, to invent, to imagine without any help or guidance other than his own intuition and judgment, a nobler aspect was imparted to his daily chore now illuminated by the radiant promise of discovery.

With his mind thus focused on the mysterious uncertainties ahead and his body seething with voluptuous fire, he grasped a pencil in trembling fingers and began charting the tortuous paths that would hopefully lead to his goal, the ideal only he could discover: Cesari's unrivaled record.

For two months after Herrick left, he drove himself, physically and mentally, performing test after test and analyzing

he results of each, allowing himself only a bare minimum
of sleep and the heroin injections essential to his equilib-
rium.

That morning, he rushed straight from his bed to the
laboratory to check on an experiment begun the previous
night. The last of a series, it contained all his hopes. With
pounding heart he entered that part of the shed reserved for
his noble endeavors.

Despite feverish impatience to begin his investigations, he had realized the necessity of a systematic approach. Bridget used to repeat it so often: order and method
are the chief assets of a research chemist—his success depends on them; even genius cannot replace them. So he
proceeded to reorganize his little kingdom, dividing it into
two autonomous laboratories, each with its own equipment
and ingredients. In one, the daily routine went forward
conscientiously, methodically—never fired, however, by
the spiritual glow inhabiting the other.

Here, the vision of discovery inspired his daytime
gropings after haunting his nightly dreams. In uttering the
words "secret of Cesari", his voice now trembled with fervor as if evoking some unknown wonder of the universe. In
this sanctuary impregnated with acetic acid vapors, he experienced the ecstasy of a painter creating a new effect of
brushwork when analysis hinted that he was progressing
and had gained a few fractions of a degree of purity in the
final poison. On the other hand, he despaired to the brink of
tears when the implacable readings told him he had retro-
gressed. But these lapses were brief and soon he was back
at work, repeating the same experiment, constantly varying
the amount of one or another constituent.

He had slept just a few hours the night before, having
gone to bed around daybreak in order to set up this experiment on which he pinned his hopes. He had stopped only

because the mixture needed to settle before he could submit it to the inexorable verdict of scientific testing. In two hours at most, he would know.

He found the laboratory in the same impeccable order he had left it. His supply of raw material—morphine—was at one end of the shed. Beyond it stood the bottle of acetic anhydride, tightly stoppered yet emitting a faint vinegary odor; a pair of scales; glass jars; and test tubes; then came the burners and the desiccator; next, the distilling apparatus with its vacuum pump, alcohol, acetate, tartaric acid, charcoal, ammonia and washing soda—all cheap and readily available commodities, as Herrick had noted, which the organization furnished him in unlimited quantity. The distiller was connected up at the intake to a sink faucet and the vile-smelling dross was carried away by an outlet hose to a nearby stream which eventually ran off into the plains.

Butler approached the container where his preparation lay waiting and lifted the cover with trembling fingers. The sight of it thrilled him. The heroin had formed a powder as fine and white as talcum. Squinting, he failed to discern any yellow trace, any sign of impurity. But the eye alone could not produce a proper verdict. He lined up his analyzing instruments and was about to begin the various steps when a frown suddenly creased his brow as he recalled that in his obsession over the experiment, he had forgotten his morning injection.

He wavered, torn between his urge to know the results of the analysis and his craving for the drug. Conscious of the fact that the test would take a while and that he would start feeling queasy within the hour, he finally resigned himself to the delay and went back to his alcove. Still, he had hesitated for several moments before deciding to sacrifice those five minutes. What prompted the choice was his fear that i

e delayed the injection, the inevitable sickish feeling
ight so disrupt his co-ordination as to jeopardize the out-
ome of the experiment.

6

LIFE DRAGGED ON drearily for Bridget after Butler's desertion. She missed him as much as she resented finding her self-appointed mission brutally interrupted when, with just a bit more patience and perseverance on his part, it might have succeeded brilliantly. Or so she told herself.

Work could not distract her from her melancholy thoughts. As head of a major department, her job entailed the same duties expected nowadays of any comparable business administrator and bore no relation to science, compelling her to function in a paper world of statistics, circulars, and reports to be read or written, which consumed her time and she detested. When these tiresome daily chores were over, she had no energy left for her own studies. Home had become a cold, forbidding shell into which she crawled listlessly to brood.

That afternoon, as she sat reading one of those insipid reports in her office adjoining the laboratory, the pout on her face translated her disgust. In a burst of annoyance, she flung the papers aside and returned to the thoughts that tormented her. What had got into Butler? Why the rupture when they were about to reach their mutual goal? In six months he had covered material that took the average stuent two years to absorb. He seemed to have acquired a enuine passion for his work. . . . As for herself, those lectures provided vital intellectual compensation for a tedious ob fast becoming unbearable.

Pondering these questions always brought her to the ame conclusion: the study program was not the cause of is desertion. This could only mean she was the cause, vhich upset her terribly. He had tired of her to the point vhere he couldn't stand having her around, couldn't stand er affection or the touch of her body. Had he ever loved er? Probably not, having thought of her merely as a life uoy to cling to while breasting the current. All she wanted vas gratitude; she had had no illusions, even before the rift. t least he could have finished his studies.

Never for an instant during their affair had she guessed is real motive for learning. She still refused to believe it, ven after what Stephens had told her. How could such a veakling find the patience and determination to imbibe all he laws of chemistry just to learn how to extract heroin? till, hadn't he fled right at the close of that chapter? No, tephens was distorting the picture. The simple truth was hat Butler couldn't stand her. Disgust must have compelled him to leave at once.

A laboratory assistant entered just as Bridget, who had aken a mirror out of her purse, was angrily contemplating he face on which sorrow had etched a decidedly ugly expression. The girl's knock had gone unacknowledged and he knew enough to expect a cool reception. Apologizing, he explained that her test results were sufficiently extraordinary to warrant informing the department head.

"What results?"

"Ninety-five percent pure heroin, Miss Dodge. I've ever seen it before."

87

Bridget started. This was a sample of a shipment re cently seized by the Narcotics Bureau—owing to a luck break, Stephens had told her without going into detail.

"Ninety-five percent? You're crazy, Jane. That's neve happened, except in France in Cesari's day. And he too the secret to his grave."

"Ninety-five percent," Jane repeated. "Here are m readings."

"I tell you it's impossible. You must have done some thing foolish, which wouldn't surprise me, like misreadin the scales."

"I can assure you. . ."

"Now I'll have to do the whole experiment again. Yo don't expect me to turn such ridiculous figures over to th Narcotics Bureau, do you? They'd think I was out of m mind."

The laboratory assistant turned and walked out, hea ing a hopeless sigh. She was young and pretty and had e dured Bridget's gusts of ill humor for several months.

Stephens was discussing their latest haul with Alle when the telephone rang. Bridget wished to give him th laboratory test results.

"It's about time," he commented jocularly, "you'r usually more prompt."

"I wanted to rerun the whole thing personally fro start to finish because my lab worker's readings seeme incredible."

Stephens noted a peculiar tremor in the voice on th other end. "Well?"

"Ninety-five percent."

He, too, started. "Ninety-five. . . Impossible! That never been done since. . . Are you positive?"

"I tell you I went over it step by step myself. I'll send you the figures if you insist. Ninety-five percent plus a tiny fraction, I'll spare you the decimals."

"That's nice of you. Now don't get angry, I believe you. Hold on a minute."

Recovered from his stupefaction, Stephens frowned and became lost in thought.

"Thanks, Bridget. This information should be very useful. By the way, as a scientist, would you happen to know how such a degree of purity can be obtained?"

She paused before answering; he could hear her tense breathing. "No registered chemist has ever achieved this record," she said at last. "I've tried myself, you know, unsuccessfully. But at least I think I discovered how to go about it—a method which entails research plus trial and error."

Stephens's frown deepened, betraying his mounting anger.

"And this method you discovered, have you kept it a secret?. . . Come now, Bridget, there's no use hedging; you know what I'm driving at. Have you rewarded a certain someone with the benefits of your knowledge and experience?"

She knew what he meant and paused to catch her breath. "I gave him a general outline," she stuttered.

Stephens raised his eyes imploringly but managed to check his indignation. What good would it do, anyway?

"Well, thanks just the same, Bridget. No, nothing else for the moment. We'll have to have a serious talk one of these days."

He hung up, then vented his rage in front of his startled assistant. "Blasted idiot!"

He told Allen about Bridget's handiwork and what he suspected. Butler had been gone for several months, had disappeared without a trace, which infuriated Stephens. Defying the Bureau's surveillance, he seemed to have vanished into thin air.

"He may have left the United States, as he told her, with a false passport. Black marketeers go in for that sort of thing. But I have good reason to suspect otherwise."

"Do you suppose they're using him as a chemist, sir?"

"Think about it. They'd be foolish not to. We know they're short of expert chemists, and along comes a former chemistry student who falls into their clutches. Not too bright perhaps, but then that idiotic girl gives him free lessons!"

Allen didn't seem entirely convinced. "That degree of proficiency takes long and patient research. How could an addict with a perfect record of failure, as you say, endure such discipline and survive? I've never heard anything like it, sir."

"Neither have I. Sometimes I wonder whether we haven't misjudged him. I only know of the fellow secondhand and it's possible that he's not as insignificant as they say. Edmund insists that each is an individual case; I ought to talk to him again about it. However, that's the province of psychology and psychiatry. To get back to the heroin we seized—frankly, I suspect it was made in this country, in some domestic laboratory."

"It's most uncommon, but I think so, too, sir."

"Why do you think so?"

"I've ordered a thorough investigation of that plane, sir. When it made a forced landing. . ."

They resumed their discussion of the incident that had been interrupted by Bridget's phone call. A plane had made an emergency landing at night in Western Pennsylvania, near the Ohio border. The damaged aircraft's pilot, uninjured and apparently the only passenger, fled into the darkess as soon as some neighboring farmers appeared. They alled the sheriff, who suspected foul play and sealed off he cockpit. When police agents examined it, they found wo bags containing a white powder they recognized as eroin.

"The plane had an auxiliary gas tank which increased ts flight range," Allen reported, "to about 600 miles; it still ad half the supply on hand when it crashed. Here are the xact figures. If full at take-off, which seems likely, the fuel onsumed by this type of aircraft, according to the experts, orresponds to a distance of 267 miles. An approximate cal-ulation, of course, there's an element of uncertainty."

"I would have figured a little less than that," Stephens iterrupted. As a licensed pilot, he had something to con-ibute in matters of aviation.

"The experts must have taken into account the strong inds along the presumed flight route that night. I sent for pies of weather reports," Allen said.

Stephens nodded approval of this meticulous attention detail, a quality he valued in his young aide. Allen drew a ap of the United States from his briefcase and spread it at on the table. He had already marked the plane's landing te in Pennsylvania. Taking a compass, he made a circle ith a radius corresponding to 267 miles.

"Look, sir, he must have taken off from a point some-here along this circle."

They huddled over the map. The circumference pene-ated large sections of Michigan and Indiana, grazed Ohio, en intersected Kentucky.

"There's no point continuing this," Allen went on. Some farmers heard the plane aloft, already in trouble, and w its lights at low altitude. Corroborative testimony from veral witnesses indicates an approximate west-east irection. . . . Incidentally, when prolonged eastward, the

91

line reaches almost straight into the heart of New York City. An important cross-check, for such a quantity of heroin must have been earmarked for the city market which is the country's biggest. The plane intended to deliver its cargo somewhere in the New York area. So I think my guess is correct."

"What guess?"

"That it took off from the region where the line intersects the western arc of my circumference: here in Indiana the northeastern portion of the state... an easy flight from Canada, you'll notice, sir, where a lot of morphine smuggling originates these days. But we're talking about heroin for the moment."

Allen ruled a line through the circle at the point in question. Stephens nodded approvingly.

"Sound reasoning, Allen, and pretty clever of them too. Our searches are generally along the coast. Do you think the laboratory is near the take-off strip?"

"I'm not sure, but of all the possibilities I've considered, it seems the most plausible. I'd like to check it out if you'll let me."

Stephens authorized the step, and Allen immediately presented him with written instructions to Indiana agents directing them to search the area with a fine-toothed comb. The narcotics chief signed the order, again noting his aide's efficiency and sense of initiative.

After her phone call, Bridget looked woebegone. Her eyes misted over at the sight of her analysis readings. Straightening her shoulders, she called her assistant—the one she had been jumping on lately, and tried to make amends.

"Your results were correct, Jane. You were right, I owe you an apology."

Ignoring the girl's polite protests, she pleaded a sudden headache, left the laboratory in charge of Jane, and rushed home to her lonely apartment where she burst into tears.

7

"YOUR INSTRUCTIONS HAVE been carried out, Fitz," Herrick reported. "The laboratory is dismantled, the shed destroyed. There's no trace of either. We sold off the remaining stock at a good price."

Fitz grunted his approval.

"It was high time; you sized up the situation perfectly."

Fitz smiled to think that anyone could doubt his ability to evaluate situations; still, it was flattering to hear his intuition praised.

"I was tipped off to hyperactive narcotics agents in northeastern Indiana."

"Not surprising after our pilot's stupid accident. They're no fools. What about Butler?"

"Safe in Canada with a new passport and papers. He can fly to Rangoon whenever you say."

"The sooner the better—next week. He has a lot of work ahead. I hope he'll do as well there as he's done here. I'm informed that everything is ready for his arrival; he can start at once."

Though the recent seizure had involved a substantial loss, Fitz had taken it in stride. He had reacted, with barely perceptible twitch of his powerful jaw, by transfer

94

ing certain funds to the profit and loss account in his personal ledger, deciding that now was the time to implement
organizational changes he had been planning for months.

The combined activities of narcotics agents and local
law enforcement had made it too risky to set up underground laboratories in France. There, only small-scale operations managed to survive—small set-ups in kitchens or
laundries with a weekly heroin output not exceeding a few
kilograms, absurdly Lilliputian in terms of Fitz's grandiose
design. Nor was the United States any safer. Though the
latest seizure stemmed from an accident, the laboratories of
a rival drug ring had also been raided and large quantities
of merchandise confiscated. Judging from the outcome of
his first experiment, Fitz resolved not to repeat what he
regarded as a tactical error. The new laboratories would
have to be located in some country beyond the Bureau's
prying eyes.

With this in mind, as he reviewed potential sites all
over the globe where the transformation of morphine into
heroin—the crux of his business—could be carried out
safely and secretly, Fitz lingered over, and finally settled
on, Burma.

That same day he confided to Herrick the reasons for
his choice. They were manifold: geographical, political,
financial—so many and so solid, in fact, that he chided himself for not thinking of it years before.

"Geographically, Herrick, it's the poppy kingdom, or
more accurately, the heart of the clandestine poppy culture.
Burma is the chief source of our raw material, and threatens
to become the sole one now that Turkey and Thailand,
under mounting American pressure, may adopt strict con-
trols. The Narcotics Bureau is extending its tentacles all
the way to there."

"But not to Burma?"

"No, not Burma, for political reasons. At least not in the hill country, the Shan States, which includes part of the golden triangle. You know about the golden triangle, don' you?"

"I've heard of it."

The words seemed to cast a spell on Fitz. He con tinued, after a pause, with rising excitement.

"There along the slopes, Herrick, surrounded b; forests teeming with elephants and yaks, massive popp; fields burst into bloom each year. Officially, the Rangoor government has banned poppy-raising, but its authorit; carries no weight above a certain altitude and probabl won't for several years to come, which is all the time I need The arms of the Narcotics Bureau don't reach that far. Have you any idea what the Shan States are like?"

Herrick had only the vaguest notion, as his work had never brought him in contact with the organization's distant operations.

"The world's most inaccessible region. Chaotic moun tain ranges 10,000-feet high in places, snow-covered it winter. Only two roads link it with China and Lowe Burma, two roads serving an area greater than 400,00 square miles! The only other transportation is on mulebac over hairpin trails defying all but experienced traveler —regions where government agents never would venture even if ordered, which is unlikely.

"The Shan tribesmen live on the upper slopes and raise a single crop, opium, their sole livelihood. Any at tempt to ban it would incite a violent revolution. The gov ernment is not about to risk that. A dream of a country!"

His voice bore a trace of romantic fervor as he went or describing the utopian region. Even Herrick found it en trancing.

"A river, the Salween; some call it the world's mos

beautiful river. A torrent high in the mountains, it fans out over several square miles when emptying into the Gulf of Martaban. Besides the Shans and several more primitive tribes—I read somewhere that headhunting still exists here—"

"You've read a lot about the country," Herrick observed.

"Almost all there is to read. Now, besides the Shans you find numerous armed tribes roaming the valleys, each with more or less defined zones of influence but occasionally warring against one another. For a variety of excuses: anti-Communist repression, Sino-Communist propaganda, Chinese nationalism—yes, remnants of Chiang Kai-shek's army hang on there. And midway up the slopes live Chinese traders waiting to snap up the harvest on the plains the moment it's in. I used to be in touch with them. But don't fool yourself, Herrick, all these gangs have a common denominator, common to the natives, the warring factions, the pirates, the smugglers, whatever their tribe may be. This denominator is opium. All the rest: Communism, anti-Communism, nationalism, or whatever, is mere talk."

"People after our own heart," Herrick commented.

"You can say that again. Opium is what incites them to quarrel, to fight, to kill each other, to trade with each other, too, when it seems to serve their interest; all this in a country which outlaws poppy culture and used to produce, just a few years ago, over 600 tons of opium annually, according to reliable estimates."

"And today?"

"No one knows for certain. Statistics are not readily available, as you can imagine. But the figure must be much higher; the most recent report I've seen. . ."

The report Fitz reached for was a typewritten, neatly bound brochure the size of a small book. As Fitz leafed

97

through it, Herrick glimpsed a succession of graphs and tables.

"According to this, the annual opium output in Upper Burma is no less than 1,000 tons."

"A thousand tons! Which yields close to 100 tons of heroin."

The figures caught Herrick's imagination as vividly as details of the landscape.

"Yes, indeed, and that's the minimum."

"I see you've gathered a lot of information on the Shan States."

"Wong sent it to me. He knows that I like to have all the facts at my fingertips."

"The Chinese in Rangoon?"

"An excellent agent. Burma has always interested me. For years I've been building solid ties there, not with petty profiteers able to send us a few dozen kilograms of inferior merchandise. Now, it's done. Wong is established in Rangoon. He's clever, reliable, a really serious worker... I pay him a lot, but he's worth it. Today, thanks partly to him, I'm in a position to contemplate a large-scale operation. Thanks also to Sanders; he's of another breed, though equally valuable."

"You mentioned him before. Isn't he the former marine sergeant?"

"That's right. A fellow who got tired of drudging for others and decided to strike out on his own, a quality I appreciate. Instead of returning to America, he settled in the Far East and went into business. Import-export... a pretext, Herrick, just another pretext. Like all the others, like Wong, it was the lure of narcotics. He started out in Thailand where he made a few contacts. We did several minor deals together through one of my agents, and now he's begging to join the organization for the great splash. A shrewd operator, but not in Wong's class. Reliable, as you'd expect an ex-marine to be. Lord knows I need dependable performers among all those pirates. I sneaked him into Burma when the Thai traffic became too risky."

"I thought the Burmese government would only grant a visitor's visa to Americans."

"Hard to obtain, but not impossible—if you can pay for it. I spare no expense for valuable agents. Sanders was already familiar with Upper Burma, especially the Shan States, where he had traveled regularly from Thailand for fresh supplies. He had set up a chain of sorts, via Bangkok, which functioned quite efficiently, I'll admit; a minuscule operation, however, out of the question nowadays. From here on we'll have to pour all our resources and efforts into Burma. Sanders is working to funnel large quantities of merchandise through the mountains to the coast. There, with Wong's help, I've arranged a feeder system to bring it here, which ought to operate smoothly, which *must* operate smoothly, Herrick," he added, a slight rasp in his voice. "It will be a big deal, a *very big* deal, bigger than anyone has ever attempted. It will succeed. You won't have a thing to do until it arrives, but you must arrange well in advance for an *extremely large* delivery."

"How large?"

Fitz looked him straight in the eye and took his time answering, as if for effect.

"Five tons of pure heroin."

8

"FIVE TONS! GOOD Lord, Fitz!"

Though accustomed to the grand scale of his em
ployer's projects, Herrick was stunned. Fitz seemed flat
tered by his stupefaction.

"In one load?"

"One load."

The figure appeared monstrous, yet Fitz obviously wa
not joking.

"Five tons of pure heroin," he continued gravely, "o
as pure as only our friend Butler can produce. Ninety-five
percent, perhaps even purer. He'll complete the local or
ganization out there. As I've been telling you all along, with
the current situation and the preparations I've made, I'c
rather attempt one bold swoop than a series of timic
passes."

"It's a tremendous risk."

"I'm the one taking the initial risk because my own
capital is invested. But it's all planned in minute detail; I've
been working on this for over a year."

"We won't be able to sell it off right away."

"You must think I'm insane. I know it has to be done
gradually. We'll stockpile it. I've arranged delivery to a

ecure warehouse. I'll tell you where shortly, for it will need prompt redistribution. That's why I mention it now. We'll provide caches in all the major cities—remember that it represents half the country's total annual consumption—and a sales force large enough to market the stuff rapidly. That's your job and it shouldn't be too difficult."

"If I'm given enough time."

"You have almost a year. I'll need that period to arrange the best and safest transport, and Butler will need it to turn out the goods."

Herrick breathed easier now. The problem began to assume manageable proportions. Fitz continued in calmer accents.

"I want you to understand my policy, Herrick. We'll disappear into our shells for a year while we prepare for the future. Our competitors can take over most of the market with the same third-rate junk they're selling right now. There will always be enough petty smuggling to keep the drug habit alive; I'll see to that. Addicts will suffer from the shortage, but this will only increase their appetite for the real thing. In a year we'll be back in business with our five tons, five tons of a premium product that will command top prices if we take the proper steps beforehand."

"Count on me," said Herrick.

"The Narcotics Bureau will be caught off guard when they discover the sudden reappearance of choice heroin. Before they can catch their breath, we'll whisk it out of sight and onto the market."

"I gather you don't intend to repeat the operation right away."

"Certainly not. We'll want to lie low afterwards, maybe for years, and even. . . if it succeeds, Herrick, and I know it will, I may never repeat it. I'll do something else."

Herrick kept silent, as if lost in thought. Actually, he was making mental calculations. At last, in a studiously nonchalant manner, he commented:

"Five tons of heroin ninety-five percent pure, after dilution say at twelve percent—which is still a superior product, deluxe as you put it—comes to nearly forty tons."

"Exactly. I figured it out long ago, as you might imagine."

"At the present retail price, it amounts to. . . impossible, Fitz!"

"About three billion dollars; your calculations are as good as mine," Fitz replied, almost in a whisper. "And it will be even more, I promise you, because the shortage will send the price skyrocketing. I'm certain of it; I had an economic expert study the question."

Herrick was speechless, stunned by the prospect. Fitz took the opportunity to remind him of several facts.

"As you yourself mentioned, I assume an enormous personal risk just by financing the raw material, which used to be a fairly modest item but no longer is. The Chinese and Burmese and Shans are not fools; they know how to count. Our friend Wong better than anyone. I'm paying four times the usual price for the opium."

Herrick performed another quick computation in his head and observed, smiling, "It still leaves an attractive margin of profit."

"Yes, and it's a good thing. With the rising cost of transport, camouflage, and pay-offs, there'll still be plenty left over for everyone."

"I'm sure. But five tons of heroin represents at least sixty tons of opium. Are you certain they have that much?"

"Do you think I walked into this blindfolded? I'm not a child, you know. Neither is Wong, nor Sanders. And the Burmese prince. . ."

"There's a Burmese prince in the picture?" Herrick gasped in amazement. These details seemed to grip his imagination like a thrilling novel.

"There's a Burmese prince. I can't tell you the whole story just yet, but believe me, I've worked out a full-scale operation over there with prominent people pulling the strings. I needed co-operation from a top local narcotics dealer, a native. The Burmese prince is probably the most dependable of the lot, at least that's what Wong and Sanders advised. What was I saying? No, the Burmese prince is no fool. High in the mountains of his primitive country, he manages to keep abreast of everything that goes on in the civilized world—at least everything related to the narcotics business. Yes, he's in it, too. Do you know he has forty tons of opium stockpiled, anticipating, as I do, a rise in price? Those forty tons are mine. I've bought them, at full price. Some of it is already converted into morphine, an operation that even unskilled natives can perform. Butler can get to work the moment he arrives, and the prince guarantees me twenty additional tons in a few months. We'll have five tons of heroin within a year."

"Such vast holdings must arouse considerable envy," Herrick observed, "in a country infested with pirates, as you say, all grabbing for opium."

"Yes, but the prince is shrewd and powerful. He keeps the stores on a mountain peak, a natural fortress more or less impregnable, according to Sanders, who lives there himself and knows all about it. This petty monarch has mercenaries on guard day and night—that's right, hired soldiers, sanctioned, occasionally supplied, by the government. Officially, he and his band are supposed to be hunting Communists. Once in a while they kill one if it serves the prince's personal interests; I've already told you what a farce *that* is. In short, an invulnerable bastion. The laboratory will be installed there; in fact it's under way right now I've already sent a list of necessary equipment and ingredients. Only the chemist is missing. It's best to centralize the operation and have only one site to defend."

"Haven't rival bands tried to steal the treasure?"

"No trouble the last I heard. Of course it costs money to buy off fractious tribes. I do it, and I'll continue doing it as long as Wong and the prince recommend it. It should suffice to discourage the fiercest among them. As for the others. . ."

"Others?"

"We'll have to fight them. That's Sanders's job, but he's a tough soldier who's seen plenty of action; he and the Burmese prince and the troops are all experienced fighters I'm told. So we're ready to face whatever happens. . . . Will you see Butler before he leaves?"

Passionately involved for months in preparing this grandiose pilot project and eager for Herrick to grasp its magnitude, Fitz had outlined the framework, enough to convey the generalities he proudly called his policy. He turned now to practical details.

"I don't think it would be advisable," Herrick replied "I feel that I ought to stay put for the moment. I've already told him what we expect of him out there. He understands and even seems enthusiastic."

"Good, I like enthusiasm," Fitz murmured.

"If you wish, I can get a message to him."

"Tell him this: we rely on him, certain that our confidence is justified. If he supplies us with those five tons of pure heroin within a year, he can rest on his laurels forever after, basking in the most exalting euphoria an addict could hope for. Tell him that success will make his fortune, and ours, and yours, Herrick."

"I'll convey the message," Herrick said, bowing.

Part
Three

1

BUTLER INJECTED HIS first dose, a fairly light one, upon rising. It would take him through the day, keep him feeling fit until the heavier evening needle—reward for the work behind him and promise of euphoric dreams to come.

He still hadn't modified his intake and was maintaining himself at the same level of consumption as when he first entered the organization. Yet, he now possessed at arm's length virtually unlimited quantities of a high-grade product. There was nothing to prevent him from helping himself to the vast stores housed on this mountain peak. No one would have noticed. He didn't do so primarily because he felt no need to, but even if the need had existed, he probably would have restrained himself out of loyalty to his employers. His promotion to a position of responsibility in the organization and the confidence won by his first achievements had conferred a new dignity on him.

After this morning ritual, he stepped outside the crude wood and bamboo hut that had lodged him for nearly a year and stood in the entrance. He had adopted the habit of allowing himself a few minutes of private contemplation in the ponderous stillness hovering at this hour over the peaks of the Shan States, gazing out at the dark chaos of mountains. The sun had not yet risen. Butler was always one of the first to stir before reveille roused the fortress garrison.

The camp, encircling a hoard of priceless goods, was perched atop the crest of a peak more than 6,000 feet above the sinuous valley of the Salween, like an ancient citadel. Sanders was right to call the place virtually impregnable, and Pyaung, the Burmese prince, had chosen to make it his headquarters. A single path allowed access, winding past steep, rugged cliffs and impassable screes defying even the hardiest mountaineers. A handful of resolute defenders could have held a battalion at bay. Still, Prince Pyaung was taking no chances and kept several hundred troops in garrison to guard the invaluable treasure. He lived there himself when not off visiting local poppy farmers or making deals with rival bands from other sectors. In addition to opium and heroin, the camp contained large stores of arms and ammunition, food, and, of course, the laboratory which was Butler's kingdom.

Only one band of marauders had dared to attack the fortress in recent months, a tribe from west of the Salween, probably lured by tales of a fabulous treasure despite the prince's efforts to amass it secretly. One night they scaled the cliffs and tried to storm the camp. A serious blunder. Pyaung liked to maintain strict discipline among his men, a policy of which Sanders heartily approved. Even when the prince was away, his orders were carried out to the letter. Security measures, developed with advice from the ex-leatherneck sergeant, worked like a charm. The alarm was sounded and the next morning seven dead bandits lay exposed on a nearby peak. For days afterwards the troops amused themselves watching hordes of vultures wheeling overhead, until all that remained was a row of blood-spattered skeletons pressed against the chalk cliffs. Word of the incident spread to other tribes in the Shan States, discouraging further raids on the Burmese prince's lair.

Butler stood plunged in a state of ecstasy, delighting in the drug's sensuous stimulation as it fanned out through his arteries to his brain. This rapture seemed of a higher order than that which he had previously experienced in dingy sheds, merging now with the majestic landscape to awaken romantic stirrings. During those fifteen minutes of contemplation each morning following the injection, he felt like a different man, capable of performing miracles.

Yet just a year before, Herrick's offer to transfer him to Burma had filled him with apprehension. Though he enjoyed his work at the time and its expanding dimensions, the very mention of the Far East had unleashed a tide of repugnant memories: the hostile, rotting jungle crawling with bloodsuckers, mosquitoes, and ants—not to mention the savage enemies lurking in the underbrush. His arrival in Rangoon did nothing to allay his dread. He felt the same old tightness gathering in his chest during those two days in the capital before they moved up into the hills. The soggy climate was painfully reminiscent of Vietnam, and the cluster of rice paddies staring at him as the plane set down, grimly recalled the dawn patrol wading through mud, sitting ducks for enemy snipers.

His mood changed once he reached the eagle's nest, where a new spirit seemed to stir him. Never before would he have let his eyes linger, as now he frequently did, on rosy peaks in the glow of dawn or on an iridescent, cascading torrent. The panoramic splendor invited such contemplation. Though Prince Pyaung had not chosen the site for its grandeur, he too was affected by it. Even Sanders, the crusty leatherneck, felt inclined to muse now and then. To the north, great masses of rock outlined the Salween's graceful valley: a chaotic chain of peaks, ridges and gulleys, steeped at the horizon in a bluish tint growing paler by degrees, beyond which the eye projected still higher, more mysterious ranges. The river, linking Tibet to the sea and splicing the Shan States up the middle, flowed approximately to the west of the hideaway which overlooked it from 3,000 feet. Butler never tired of hunting out its crystal traces which sparkled through the dense undergrowth covering the banks. No misty overcast shrouded the sunlight; nothing like the milky whiteness of the tropical plain. Here, the air was fresh and cool; the nights, often frigid, were always starry in the dry season. "The valley of the Salween brings bad luck to outsiders," Sanders used to say. Butler merely smiled now when he heard this.

The opaque inky blueness marking the end of night began to splinter into a sheaf of changing hues along the mountain tops. This morning, as usual, Butler's meditation was shattered by the clamor of reveille. The soldiers' barracks just below the summit formed a solid ring around the laboratory and the narcotics stores they were guarding—a hoard the nature of which they surely knew as well as the fact that it was priceless, though just how fabulously priceless in Western eyes they never could have imagined.

Prince Pyaung recruited his men carefully, paid and fed them well. All were young Shans, mostly from the hill tribes. Their fathers cultivated poppy, which for generations had been the sole source of their meager income. Life was hard for these farmers. Before planting could begin, they had to struggle against the forest, burn down trees, strip away stumps, clear the land, and after two or three harvests had impoverished the soil, they had to move on in search of virgin earth. Each year, Chinese traders living in the foothills, acting as middlemen between the farmers and the wholesalers in Rangoon, climbed the slopes to buy the poppy yield, averaging twenty to twenty-five pounds of opium per family. The shabby price they paid, equivalent to fifteen or twenty dollars per pound, often took the form of barter—salt, cloth, or saucepans—offered at exorbitant values. On top of that, they would lend out money for which they charged from ten to twenty percent monthly interest.

The sons turned their backs on farming and provided Pyaung with most of his recruits. Being half-Shan, half-Thai himself, the prince understood them and was able to impose his authority. As soldiers in his miniature army they found life less precarious than did their parents, being assured of enough rice to eat and pocket money to spend when furloughed briefly to their native hamlets. They never grumbled about having to live on this remote peak. Some of the married men received permission to bring along their families, who camped a short distance from the fortress, ready to dash for safety in case of an alert. Those who went on leave returned promptly when expected, creating an efficient rotation system.

Butler, for one, had not set foot outside the camp in the year since his arrival, the laboratory having demanded his constant attention. Yet, he never complained. As in Indiana, his daily work and an unchanging dose of heroin kept him from feeling lonely. He lost no sleep over Bridget's absence.

2

THE SUN BEGAN to redden the peaks, signaling the close of his self-allotted daily recreation spell. He strode briskly toward the laboratory.

Below, the barracks were coming to life as a cheerful commotion rose up the mountain. He stopped to observe a ritual that took place every morning at the same hour, the flag-raising ceremony. Stifling a smile, he stood at attention, conscious of being watched. A dozen soldiers in the same dull-colored uniforms raucously chanted what sounded like a patriotic ode while one of them hoisted a flag to the tip of a long bamboo pole wedged between two rocks. Neither flag nor anthem was Burma's official one; Butler had no idea which state or group or tribe they represented, and some of the soldiers may have shared his ignorance. But Prince Pyaung attached great importance to the daily rite, which was observed with unfailing solemnity in this eagle's nest overlooking the River Salween by members of a community who, on different levels, were all active participants in the satanic drug trade. A man of the world, Prince Pyaung insisted on order and discipline in his little kingdom. Fitz admired his organizing abilities and other talents that he had heard about in detailed reports from Wong.

Similar rituals were taking place at the same hour in other regions of Upper Burma, involving officiants of various ancestry: Karens, Kachins, Lahus, Palangs, Was, Chinese, and members of certain sects designated only by initials, all wearing the same uniforms, raising different flags, singing different anthems in the dozen or more tongues of rival tribes populating this part of the globe, among whom, as Fitz had pointed out, the single common bond was opium—opium plus the assorted poisons which centuries of Asian experience have succeeded in extracting from it and Western science has refined to the utmost.

"At ease!" snapped a sarcastic voice behind Butler.

Butler didn't resent finding Sanders up and around earlier than usual. A year of living together, the only whites in this fortress cloister, had improved their relationship.

Their first contact had been rather shaky. The pseudonym under which messages from the organization had introduced Butler meant nothing to the sergeant until he went to fetch him in Rangoon and instantly recognized the wretched G.I. whose shameless cowardice on a patrol mission in Vietnam Sanders held largely responsible for the loss of a convoy, a partial massacre, and the sergeant's own injury.

Cursing the fellow roundly in his own colorful expletives, he promised himself a stormy showdown at the first opportunity. And no less embittered at the prospect of having to face, for at least a year, the brutish superior whose humiliations still festered, Butler suffered a shock violent enough to necessitate extra doses of heroin during the two days in Rangoon. Sanders realized this and became doubly aggressive. He hated and despised drug addicts though his current occupation tended to aid and abet their vice. Wong's timely intervention and soothing influence averted a clash. On the eve of their departure for the hills, while Butler remained locked in his room, Sanders explained the situation to the Chinese and vented his rage.

"A junkie! That's the kind of help they send us! Ignorant as ever about this country. They don't realize what kind of man it takes to survive here." He sounded like a colonial planter or lumberman complaining about the senseless hiring policies formulated in Western councils by the snug residents of luxury apartments, surrounded with all the comforts and refinements of civilized living, totally unaware of the primitive conditions under which the recruits would have to work.

Wong smiled and tried to reason with him. "Opium needs chemists. Excellent reports about the gentleman as chemist. Ninety-five percent. Exceptional."

Wong, who had lived in both Hong Kong and the United States, spoke good English with a creditable accent but used no more words than were absolutely essential to make himself understood. Sanders shrugged his shoulders, his combativeness reinforced by Rangoon's oppressive heat after the invigorating mountain air to which he had grown accustomed. He never visited the capital except to confer with Wong, exchange news of the camp for Wong's news from the organization, and spend a couple of nights with a prostitute. He couldn't wait to get back to the mountain.

"Not just an addict, but a coward as well." Feeling the urge to share his indignation and disgust with someone, he recounted the Vietnam incident, concluding with a prediction: "If anything should happen at the camp, if he should feel threatened, I know he'll run like a rabbit."

"Cannot run far up there," Wong observed archly.

114

"True," Sanders admitted. "Still, he's the last buddy I'd have chosen if anyone had bothered to ask me."

"Two lone white men thrown together in close quarters for a year ought to become friends at once," Wong observed with an emphatic nod.

Sanders spent the whole night reflecting on this judicious remark, for he valued Wong's advice. The next morning, just before leaving, he held out his hand to Butler. "I'm willing to let bygones be bygones, old pal. If you put your mind to it, maybe we can get along."

Butler was only too happy to forget the past. Sanders managed to control his hostility afterwards and gradually adjusted to his company. Much to the sergeant's surprise, he found that Butler's addiction didn't prevent him from working industriously at his trade and began to treat him as a friend. Once in a while, however, when suddenly reminded of Vietnam, Sanders would reveal his contempt for Butler's past conduct, but in time those flare-ups grew more rare.

"At ease! The circus is over!" Sanders repeated.

He never missed a chance to poke fun at the flag-raising ceremony, but while it was happening and despite the fact it meant nothing to him, he always stood stiffly at attention, which vouched for his long record of army service. Below them, the soldiers returned to their posts.

"I've received a message from Wong," Sanders said. "Everything's ready on his end. Departure in three weeks."

A small transmitter kept them in touch with Rangoon. Sanders, who had been something of a jack-of-all-trades since leaving the army, operated it.

"I hope you'll be ready, too."

"Inside of two weeks. I haven't much more to process. We'll get our five tons. . . the last couple of hundred pounds at ninety-eight percent," Butler asserted, his eyes burning, "the rest at ninety-five or ninety-six; that's the best I could do."

"No call for apologies, old pal," said Sanders, clapping him on the back. "Perfection is for the next world."

3

IT WAS TRUE: several weeks earlier, as a result of experiments conducted in these tranquil surroundings so conducive to research and speculation, he had attained a degree of purity unmatched by King Cesari himself.

"Want to see a sample of my product?"

Sanders trusted his proficiency, but Butler's "*my product*" rang with such pride that the sergeant didn't have the heart to refuse. The two stepped into the laboratory.

Its shell, unlike the flimsy huts they lived in, consisted of double rows of hardwood posts driven deep into the ground and bound together to form a solid wall. The narrow windows were barred, the door bolted and padlocked; only Butler and Sanders had keys. Two of the prince's bodyguards stood watch day and night outside the building. Only the chemist entered, or occasionally Sanders or Pyaung, in addition to Butler's regular helper, a feeble-minded deaf-mute named Gyi, the young Shan assigned by the prince to do the heavy work. A former cook's assistant, he had no trouble making the switch from kitchen kettles to laboratory vessels. Butler assigned him only the muscular chores and Gyi was searched at the close of each work day.

The massive door shut behind them, screening out the mounting hubbub from the yard outside. This laboratory was as tidy and well organized as the one in Indiana, bu much more spacious. Butler's immediate problem on arriv al had been to figure out how to extract five tons of heroin within a year, or about 200 pounds weekly, not far short o industrial production levels. For a while he was obliged to suspend his theoretical experiments on quality control in order to organize this massive output, which was no easy feat with only one inexperienced helper. Buckling to the task with renewed vigor, he finished it in no time, proving once again his unfailing resourcefulness and ingenuity doubling, then tripling his chain of apparatus, observing rules inspired by Taylor's ghost, laws he had never heard o yet stumbled on one by one as he went along, driven by necessity and the lure of discovery. In Rangoon, Wong ex erted himself with typical efficiency to provide additiona raw material as it was needed.

The water supply worried Butler at first, a touchy prob lem for the camp even before his arrival. Every day a mule train set out under heavy escort to bring fresh water from a mountain stream feeding into the Salween several hundred yards below. But Butler wasn't satisfied with the few bar rels they delivered; the laboratory demanded greater quan tities. Furthermore, he needed running water and called for construction of a cistern atop the summit, to be filled up every day even if it meant quadrupling the fatigue squads.

Prince Pyaung needed coaxing at first. The Chinese chemists he had once seen working in a dilapidated shanty, using old tin cans for containers, had not demanded such luxury. But after Sanders assured him that this was an en tirely different operation, Wong used all his influence, and that of the organization backing him, to meet Butler's re quest. With bags of cement sent out from Rangoon, the sol diers constructed a cistern under Sanders's direction, and soon running water began to flow through bamboo piping.

he sergeant took this opportunity to install showers in his, utler's, and the prince's huts. It helped to diminish 'yaung's resentment at seeing his soldiers transformed into 1asons.

Having completed his production quota in a few /eeks, Butler returned to his qualitative experiments. It ook him several months to achieve the results he was se- retly aiming for, but at last he did. He set a new record, far uperior to Cesari's.

Look at this, Sanders. My latest efforts. It hasn't been acked yet. Have you ever laid eyes on choicer goods?"

He plunged both hands into a container half-filled with chalky powder resembling fine-sifted flour. Sanders hought of a miser running his fingers through a hoard of old pieces.

"Not a spot, not a tinge, not a speck."

The sergeant's polite admiration bore a trace of sar- asm. He, like Herrick, was forever amazed, and occasion- lly moved, by this addict's behavior. He walked over to he area reserved for storing the finished product which it vas his job to convoy through the mountainous Shan States. The transportation problem was the real issue in his eyes— ar more crucial than a few fractions of a percentage up or lown the scale—a problem that he and the Burmese prince ad been studying daily for months without yet having re- noved all the hazards.

The heroin was packed in ordinary rice sacks covered ver with protective plastic wrappers. Both Sanders and 'yaung had agreed that further camouflage was pointless n the trip through the mountains. Any official inspection vould inevitably reveal the treasure, and their job was to ee that no such mishap occurred.

119

Sanders reached out to pat some of the sacks.

"I've checked to make sure all the wrappers are tight," Butler said, "and weighed them too—sixty-five pound apiece."

"Good. Two sacks per mule. Light enough, but the trail is long and rough. It's better not to overload them. All told 167 sacks."

"And here are 160 filled and ready to go. I'll have the rest in ten days. The last ten will contain the batch that' ninety-eight percent."

"You'll have to mark it," Sanders murmured absently "Our people may want to single it out."

"I've done that already. See, a tiny cross, barely notice able." He was not about to let his masterpiece get mixed i with all the rest.

Sanders smiled condescendingly. "Good. We'll pu them on the surest-footed animals. So that'll mean abou eighty-five mules plus replacements and a few extra fo baggage, between 110 and 120 animals. That's what I wa planning on. A long caravan, Butler," he added pensively "They've been used before in these parts, over even longe trails, but never over such rough trails for such a grea distance."

"How far is it?"

"Nearly 600 miles through treacherous country. Som animals will die on the way; maybe some men will, too."

"Men? You mean there's a risk of. . ."

"Fighting? Listen, Butler, for about a month's time we're going to be transporting priceless merchandise—a treasure we haven't been able to hide—through a regio swarming with bandits, or worse still, self-styled soldiers Don't think it's going to be a joy ride. True, some of th tribes have been bought off by Pyaung—God bless him another pirate who's been paid enough to do just that! Som

tribes can be relied on not to interfere, even if they won't
co-operate. But there are others who can't be trusted. And
even though we're taking back trails, no train of 120 mules
is going to pass unnoticed. Besides, I can't see what difference it makes to you," he burst out impatiently. "While
we're sweating and fighting in the brush, you'll be strutting
around like a peacock in New York, showered with praise
from the organization for your ninety-eight percent and
with a fancy bonus, I'll bet—not that you don't deserve it."

In fact, plans had been made to return Butler, once his
work was finished, to Rangoon on the Sino-Burmese road
and thence by plane to the United States. Destruction of the
laboratory and its equipment was also projected.

"By the way, I'd like to ask you. . . "

"What?"

"To let me join the expedition," Butler stated firmly.

Sanders stared at him, dumfounded. Recovering his
voice, he retorted crossly, "Don't you think we have troubles enough with a 120-mule train? You want to add on
more dead weight?"

"Look, Sanders, I'm sure I can help you."

"You'll probably have to fight," said the sergeant, eyeing him mercilessly.

"I'll fight if I have to. I want to see this thing through."

Sanders was nonplussed. "Look, old pal," he began,
his voice softening, "I don't want to hurt your feelings, but I
once saw what kind of fighter you. . ."

Butler interrupted with unwonted authority. "This
situation is different. Deep down, I know that I can help. I
want to go along."

"You. . . *want* to?"

Sanders seemed more dismayed than angered by this
change of heart. He scratched his ear, undecided. "As far as
I'm concerned, it's no great problem. Just one more mule.

121

But my orders come from the top and they say you go di rectly to Rangoon."

"Send a message to Wong and let him submit my re quest to the organization."

Shut up in his laboratory and absorbed in his dail work for a whole year, Butler never gave a thought to th matter of transportation. Only during the past few days ha it begun to haunt him as he imagined the hazardous journe that awaited the treasure he had so patiently amassed.

After Sanders finally promised to convey his request t their superiors, Butler, now further emboldened, plied th sergeant with questions about the route they would tak and especially about security measures. These queries ha the unique effect of arousing the sergeant's ill temper.

"If by some chance you're allowed to come with us, i doesn't mean you can stick your nose in other people's busi ness. You'll be dumped on the back of a mule and you'll g where he goes. Dammit, once in a while I wouldn't min being in your shoes. And you better get it straight from th start that you've got nothing to say. I'm running the show with Prince Pyaung. Security? You mean in case of ambus or attack? Well, you just scuttle your mule and crawl into hole in the rocks with your head between your hands unti the fighting's over. If your nerves get too shaky in the mean time, take double or triple doses of your poison, but stay ou of my hair. That's the best advice I can give you."

Butler hung his head, unmindful of the sarcasm. Onc again the sergeant's voice softened and he patted him o the back.

"Each to his own trade, old pal; fighting is mine You've done your job and done it well. Now let me d mine—ours, Pyaung's and mine. He and his boys know what they're up to; I've seen them go at it. Fighting's no your business. Understand? Anyway, if you want, I can ti ou off to the worst hazards we're likely to meet. The prince will be back from his tour soon. He'll have handed out more baksheesh and collected the latest news. We have to sit down together to map out the final details and then plan our campaign. You can come to the conference, if you're interested, as long as you don't try to tell us what to do."

"I'll be there," Butler promised, raising his head.

4

PYAUNG CAME BACK several days later from the reconnai
sance mission preceding the general departure—a long an
exhausting journey involving last-minute wheeling an
dealing with various local tribes over which he exerted cor
siderable influence. The prince descended from an ancie
and powerful family that once ruled a large portion of th
Shan States, including its richest valleys. Over the yea
this influence had dwindled; now he was slowly rebuildir
it, at least in the mountains, with an eye to controlling th
poppy farmers and the petty profiteers who flock to ther

On his return, he took a day off to rest and medita
over a pipe of opium. Like many Asians, Pyaung looke
upon heroin use as an exercise in barbarism and felt th
practitioners of this vice deserved the contempt of wir
connoisseurs for liquor lovers. He indulged in a pipe or tv
of opium during leisure hours, but never smoked on activ
duty.

He stayed in his hut, stretched on the couch, aft
changing to a sarong and an embroidered silk jacket, h
preferred costume when he considered himself off-dut
On duty, he wore the same outfit as his soldiers: bei
trousers and tunic, a visored cap, and sandals, the regul
uniform of all armed bands and their leaders throughout tl

Shan States. The only attributes that set him apart from the others were his relative height, his authoritative gestures, and the cut of his hair, which he, unlike his men, wore long and never bothered to tuck up under his cap.

He had shaken hands with Sanders on arrival, and, without a word about his trip, arranged to confer with him the following evening. The sergeant asked no questions and made no attempt to see him beforehand. He was familiar with the prince's habits and respected them.

Pyaung rose early the next morning and heard his adjutant's report of events and conditions in camp during his absence. Then he inspected his troops and spent the rest of the day attending to matters that concerned him. In the evening, after a light meal, he put on his fleece-lined Chinese overcoat—for the night air was cold—and went over to Sanders's hut to discuss the coming expedition.

"It is over 600 miles through the mountains," Pyaung said. "We must cross the entire Shan States and part of Tenasserim. An arduous journey through ravines and over torrents. I expect it will take a month or more."

"That's a long time. But Wong knows all about it and won't look for us beforehand. I assume you still feel it's the safest way. So we'll take it."

"I am convinced it is the only way this large a convoy can go."

Hunched over a full-scale map of Burma spread out on the table, the prince finished penciling in the proposed route, which Sanders examined critically. Behind them, peering over their shoulders, seemingly ignored, Butler listened attentively but took no part in the discussion. Sanders's hut, of wood and bamboo like all the rest, contained a bed, a table, and three wobbly chairs. The former leatherneck sergeant kept his Spartan premises in impeccable order. Each morning he pulled his bedding apart, shook it out, and made sure that a soldier swept the rush mat covering the pebbly floor. This kept rats and insects at bay, unlike other huts where the braziers attracted all kinds of crawling and flying things. The only decorative touches were a snapshot of a smiling girl in tennis clothes whom Sanders had known somewhere back in the distant past, which he kept around for no particular reason, and, at the head of his cot, some nude cut-outs of movie stars from the Rangoon magazines. On one and all, Sanders turned an occasional longing gaze.

The air was warm. A wood fire burned on an earthen hearth in the center of the room. Smoke spiraled up haphazardly through outlets pierced in the roof (hastily plugged up in the event of rain) and through chinks in the ill-fitting wall boards. The residual clouds didn't seem to bother the men, who were used to them and too engrossed in planning the coming adventure to be distracted by physical inconveniences. Having tossed aside his coat as he entered, Pyaung resembled a prince of ancient times in his richly-embroidered silk coat trimmed with gold and ornate turban studded with ancestral jewels.

"The only way this large a convoy can go," he repeated.

During the previous year, several plans had been studied for transporting the merchandise to the coast—the first stage of its trip to the drug-devouring West—and subsequently abandoned as a result of information culled by the prince in the Shan States or by Wong in Rangoon. As the campsite was approximately 100 miles east of Lashio, the simplest solution at first seemed to call for dispatching the mule train in that direction, crossing the Salween, and then picking up the famous Burma Road—the only road in the

126

entire region wide enough to accommodate commercial vehicles. Transferred onto trucks, the merchandise would proceed to Rangoon via Mandalay. This was the fastest route, frequently used for all types of smuggling in the past and currently used by small-time opium traffickers. The latter, however, were compelled to buy off civil and military officials stationed all along the way. After putting out feelers, Pyaung had concluded that the cost of paying out hush money for a shipment whose size the whole countryside was beginning to guess would be prohibitive; astronomical, and without any real assurance of safe conduct. For similar reasons, Wong felt it was too risky to ship the goods from any port in the vicinity of Rangoon where the semiautonomy of the hill regions ceased to operate and the relative strength of central authority might undo the whole operation. So they gave up the idea of trucks and the Burma Road.

Other alternatives were debated and found wanting, until the only reasonable plan turned out to be the wild 600-mile trek southward through the mountains of the Shan States—a formidable obstacle course owing to the rugged terrain, one of the most inaccessible regions on earth, and, for that very reason, unlikely to attract bandits. The odyssey would end near the coast, but not too close—at some point along the banks of the Salween where Wong would arrange to have the goods loaded onto a Chinese junk and taken up the river beyond the densely populated rice-growing sector.

Sanders silently studied the charted route. Its north-south direction roughly paralleled the Salween, with frequent detours necessitated by factors that Pyaung explained as he pointed them out on the map.

"Here, a torrent too wide to ford. We have a steep climb before we can get across. Over there is Lahu headquarters; we do not get along. Impossible to bribe them. We must loop around. But even if we avoid their main force we can expect to encounter patrols which they send out quite far in all directions. They are well armed and good fighters."

This vision of rushing torrents, of scaling misty mountain ridges, leaping across chasms, and above all the promise of battle, seemed to enthrall Sanders who nodded approvingly as he memorized these critical points with a concentrated effort that etched a frown on his forehead. The Burmese prince seemed equally absorbed.

Staring at the map by the light of a kerosene lamp hanging from the roof, Butler listened no less avidly, straining his ears to catch every detail. Despite the offhand treatment meted out to him by the two others, he knew for certain now that this adventure was to be partly his. First Sanders, then Wong had sent on his request to join the expedition, and Fitz, after discussing it with Herrick, had not seen fit to deny it. "After all, the fellow has been a great asset wherever we've sent him, Herrick. Maybe he'll prove his usefulness once again. Might as well let him go if that's what he wants."

"Particularly since Sanders seems willing," said Herrick, to whom Fitz had shown the message.

Stemming from a change of heart that eluded his own understanding, and with much vacillating and cursing, Sanders had yielded to some obscure impulse and finally gave in.

On learning that his request was granted, Butler experienced the same joyful surge that had heralded his entrance into laboratory research back in Indiana; the same euphoric glow, the same rapturous sensation of bounding up to greater heights, the same feverish excitement, translated by the same exuberant energy. By working through

128

art of the night and relentlessly prodding his helper, the eaf-mute Gyi, he did a week's work in three days and ompleted the production of five tons of the purest heroin, rowning the task that had absorbed him body and soul for nore than a year.

From that moment on, his hopes and dreams took a ew turn.

5

FRANTIC AS HE had been in recent weeks over the though
that his choicest powder, the fruit of his labor, would be
exposed to dire peril in transit and he could do nothing to
protect it, he began to feel less alarmed, oddly enough
about the hazards of the expedition once he was certain o
joining it. His intense curiosity about this prodigiously
challenging odyssey swept fear from his troubled spirit.

This interest, verging at times on enthusiasm, neve
once flagged as his two companions began to relate (in de
tail and with relish) the obstacles, the exhausting marches
and the ambushes which they seemed to anticipate hun
grily like gluttons on the eve of holiday feasting.

This state of mind was new to him. During the pas
year, whenever the three of them had happened to get to
gether for an evening over a bottle of liquor, the conversa
tion invariably turned into an exchange of war stories be
tween Sanders and Pyaung. The fearless jungle fighter and
the bandit chief who had spent his life defending and ex
tending his mountain turf, delighted in trading tales. Tale
of violence for the most part, which sent chills up Butler'
spine and gave him nightmares. Sanders, the more talkative
of the pair, drank a lot without ever showing it, and cheered
by the first few gulps, began reeling off his past exploit

with decidedly wistful fervor: night patrols, hand-to-hand struggles, mopping up snipers' nests with flame-throwers and machetes. The ending was always bloody, the slaughter depicted in gory detail, as if he took a kind of sadistic pleasure in shocking Butler's morbid sensibilities and couldn't resist breaking the truce between them in order to make an implicit declaration of his own superior courage.

The prince was more reticent. He listened and said nothing, yet his expression conveyed rapt attention, or enthusiasm, depending on the anecdote. In turn, he would relate his own adventures which sounded equally sinister to Butler, who suspected that the two were secretly pledged to terrorize him. This wasn't true, though an unwritten pact achieved the same result: the unity and complicity of courage in the face of cowardice. For Pyaung knew Butler's weaknesses, and if Oriental restraint kept him from exposing his contempt for the chemist, his excessively polite manner often was more insulting.

These conferences—rare as they were, fortunately —became so distressing that he started taking double doses of heroin just beforehand to erase the repelling images. His tremors ceased, but the barrage of boastful chatter filled him with exasperation and droned on tediously, detracting from the heroin's intoxicating bliss.

Tonight he reacted very differently. The bold new spirit within him refused to be cowed by their usual gory tales. The pair neither frightened nor wearied him. After a pause, broken only by the faint sputtering of the lamp, he ventured a sudden remark addressed to Pyaung. "The torrents familiar to you, prince, may not be so familiar when our caravan gets there. The rains are likely to start soon."

Pyaung looked up sharply, his long hair bobbing. The comment startled him because it echoed his own concern. The expedition had been postponed to allow for certain arrangements Wong had to make, and he worried about the risk of early rains.

"Correct," he nodded, "but I am not to blame if we leave later than I advised. Anyway, I considered this possibility, and wherever the water is too deep, we will move on until we reach one of many vine-woven bridges spanning these mountain streams, which the guides know about. The men will unload the mules and carry the packs across. The mules will have to swim; it won't be the first time."

"I've heard," Butler volunteered again, matter-of-factly, "that certain streams can rise as much as fifty feet —the Salween, for instance."

"Even higher, but only in the rainy season. At any rate we ought to leave."

"We ought to leave," Sanders echoed.

"Yes, we ought to leave, that's for certain," Butler chimed in. "I just thought it would be best to expect the worst, though I'm sure you planned for everything, prince."

Sanders and Pyaung exchanged furtive glances. Sensing that his comment had had a certain impact, Butler maintained a posture and a tone of self-assurance. The two chiefs continued their conference, but now and then the prince would look at Butler as if to ask his opinion.

They reviewed the most dangerous stage of the journey, through Lahu territory, and Butler spoke up again. "I I understand you correctly, in case of trouble there'll be no question of our paying a toll."

"No such deal is possible with the Lahus."

"And there's bound to be trouble?"

"Almost certainly," the prince replied.

"That means a fight. Almost certainly, as you put it."

Butler's voice was calm and objective without a trace of apprehension. Impossible, thought Sanders. This man who feared violence like the plague, whose face clouded over a the mention of fighting, was now talking of battle without batting an eyelash. He must have taken a triple shot of heroin before coming here.

The sergeant would have been astounded to learn that Butler had, in fact, taken no drug at all, having postponed his evening injection in order to allow every last detail concerning the expedition to be inscribed in a clear and lucid mind. Sanders would have been even more astounded to know that even at this late hour, physical and emotional stability accompanied the weaning process instead of the frantic anxiety characteristic of addicts in need of drug.

"Almost certainly," the prince repeated solemnly, with the same probing stare. "Some may be wounded, some may die. I have planned for this, too. We will take whatever is needed to dress wounds. As for the dead. . . my men are trained to fight."

"I wasn't thinking of the soldiers, prince," said Butler; "on that score, I know your plans are perfect. But some of the mules may get injured or killed. Don't you think we ought to have extras, Sanders, to step in and take up the load?"

Disconcerted still further by Butler's self-assurance, Sanders didn't even think to snap at the implied criticism. Pyaung answered instead.

"I was worried about that *also,* Mr. Butler," he said softly, "but 120 mules are all we can find in this area. Rest assured, though; I have inquired all along our route and found out where we can replace our losses either by purchasing animals at a reasonable price or. . ."

The idea was too obvious to require further words. Butler nodded, satisfied with the reply, and the lamplight conference, now a trio, continued as Butler took an increasingly active role unchallenged by the others.

It was very late when he returned to his hut after making his usual rounds of the silent laboratory to check that the guards were not dozing. He went to sleep so engrossed in thoughts of the past evening that he forgot to take his injection, his passport to blissful serenity. Not for an hour, until just before daybreak, did he realize it with the onset of spasms, and he rushed out of bed to repair the oversight. Up to that point the impending adventure had enticed him into a dream world radiant enough to outshine his artificial paradise.

6

"BURMA'S FLATLANDS PRODUCE rice, Mr. Fitz—not as much as they once did, but enough to export a small quantity to Malaya. Rice sacks will provide the least suspicious wrappers for the first part of the journey."

The conversation was taking place in Wong's office in Rangoon, the last stop on Fitz's Far Eastern tour. Though booked as a pleasure trip, its real purpose was to allow a private chat with the Chinese agent. Fitz trusted him up to a point, and, like all drug moguls, made it his practice to stay clear of the theater of operations. But this affair was so important and meant so much to him that he felt compelled to spur on the key members of his organization.

To avoid attention, he toured the East Indies first, stopping at various Indonesian Islands, Malaya, and Thailand before visiting Burma. There, accompanied by his mistress of the moment, he performed splendidly as a wide-eyed tourist eager to take in the local sights. The girl was delighted to travel to places she had never even heard of and went on with him to Mandalay, Moulmein, and other ancient cities much touted by the travel bureaus. Upon golden pagodas he cast a hopelessly indifferent eye, which somehow managed to convey blissful admiration. In Rangoon at last, he called on the Chinese while his companion, exhausted by the city's oppressive heat, took a nap.

Wong had trafficked here and there all over Southeast Asia; in Vietnam, Thailand, Laos, and Hong Kong, and had also lived for a short time in the United States where he and Fitz originally met and mounted the present operation. He had mastered the art of adapting his conversational manner to suit the person to whom he was talking. With Chinese compatriots he maintained the leisurely, roundabout approach of his ancestors; but with Westerners, he drove straight to the point. He knew Fitz liked his directness and Fitz was paying him—royally.

"Owner of the junk is a reliable man, a Chinese. Makes a business of transporting black-market rice to Malaya, near Penang, without passing through customs. He did it for me once, routine job. I said and he believes this is more rice. Better that way; keeps the price down."

"Right," Fitz nodded. "So the junk sails up the Salween to where the hills begin. . . ."

"Just beyond there; region not so populated; river still navigable far from the sea."

". . . and waits for the caravan. The goods are loaded onto the junk. Then what?" Fitz knew the general framework of the next stage but wanted Wong to spell out all the details.

"Junk sails slowly down the river, passing Moulmein. One customs boat. They always ignore this junk; routine job. I have paid; no more than usual; for rice. The rate for rice, Mr. Fitz," and here he wagged his head emphatically, "is much lower than for drugs. Secret and cheap: two advantages."

This mode of reasoning could not fail to appeal to Fitz, who nodded approvingly.

"Junk heads out to sea bound for Malaya, a point just

north of Penang. Long trip, over 600 miles, but faster than mule ride through mountains, Mr. Fitz. Less than a week. The captain knows many small islands where he can anchor and no one looks."

"What about in Malaya itself?"

"Harder to organize in Malaya, more costly too. It was necessary to share our secret with plantation manager."

"I know. Can he be trusted?"

"He is Anglo-Chinese friend of mine," Wong replied solemnly.

Fitz felt satisfied with this statement. The junk trip from Burma to Malaya was the second leg of the operation. The third, the shipment to the United States, had occasioned lengthy research and reflection. Wong himself had come up with the solution they ultimately adopted. Fitz reminded him of this and asked if he foresaw any complications.

"I have studied all phases of the problem, Mr. Fitz. The safest way. I thought so; I still think so."

Wong never involved himself in an affair before studying it seriously. When he was in the United States and Fitz had sought his advice about shipping an abnormally large quantity of narcotics, he began by compiling a small library on the various methods used to smuggle contraband through customs. The list was endless, like the disguises: toothpaste tubes, toilet cases, canned goods, cameras, underwear, fake bandages, fake hunchbacks, fake pregnancies—for small or moderate quantities; refrigerators, rigged-up autos, specially designed boats—for larger loads. During the Vietnam War, even the coffins of American G.I.s came into use—the bodies slit open and sewn up again, serving as containers.

After reviewing "all phases of the problem," as he put it, and smoking a pipe or two of opium to clarify his

137

thoughts, Wong had decided that none of these disguises would do for so large a cargo. Anyway, the customs people knew them all and would be on the lookout. It would be best to bring in the heroin under the label of some common, regularly imported product.

Once back in Rangoon, he made a survey of the cargoes shipped by freighter out of various Southeast Asian ports to the United States. This was easy enough since his business in recent years had required him to cultivate good relations with all the export brokers. He sifted through lists of commodities and rejected them all for one reason or another. He wanted a plain everyday product common enough not to attract comment, yet bulky enough to encase the heavy contraband. The results of his survey were absorbed into the current plan: shipment in rice sacks from Burma to Malaya, then concealment of the heroin in heavy bales of rubber produced on Pará rubber plantations and routinely shipped to the West from Penang or Singapore.

After examining and approving the plan, Fitz arranged for delivery to the United States. He did this with the same enterprising spirit characteristic of his approach to all business matters, not hesitating to acquire a tire factory more than a year before the current operation got under way, while the idea was still incubating. The factory was near bankruptcy; inside a few months he had it back on its feet under new management, making money, and fast acquiring recognition for high-grade products. Like all such plants, it periodically received large shipments of sheets of rubber pressed into bales which originated in tropical countries where the Pará rubber tree grows.

During the conference in Rangoon, Fitz wanted to make certain that every detail had been arranged. This seemed to be the case from what Wong told him.

"The sacks of 'rice' are unloaded north of Penang, trucked to one of the plantation warehouses where only two men work, both trustworthy. My friend the manager has built up large reserves of sheets of rubber. The heroin is placed in specially designed containers, also made of rubber, and a bale of the usual size and weight is formed around it, then sent on to the pressing machine, and stamped and ticketed with the plantation's well-known label."

"How much heroin per bale?"

"Fifty-five pounds. That leaves a good thick width of rubber. The ordinary bale weighs about 220 pounds."

"Forty for a ton of drugs makes two hundred in all," Fitz calculated. "Twenty tons of rubber is about the normal size of a shipment from the plantation."

"That's correct, and not by coincidence, Mr. Fitz," the Chinese replied with a faint smile. "Twenty tons of rubber, two trucks. . . trucks that leave the plantation with their registered load the day preceding the shipment—my friend must keep a strict count—bound for Penang. Only they will stop overnight in the warehouse where the substitution will be made."

"But that calls for a work crew," Fitz exclaimed in alarm, "more people in on the secret."

"Only two I said, Mr. Fitz, two well-paid men. My friend sees to everything. The warehouse is equipped with the latest hoisting equipment."

"And the truck drivers?"

"Will know nothing. They won't suspect the substitution which will be done while they sleep."

The whole operation fit together neatly. Wong added a few more details; he seemed to have thought of everything.

"Daylight departure from Penang, the same bales of

rubber that go out every week, numbered and stenciled, giving plantation of origin and address in America."

"The same way we intend to unload it in New York," said Fitz, "in broad daylight. The rest is my worry."

"Papers in order, valid certificates, nothing can match this operation," Wong concluded, rubbing his hands. "All will go well, I am sure, Mr. Fitz."

"All will go well indeed if the mule train reaches the coast safely," Fitz said with a trace of anxiety. "That, I think, is the worst phase of the trip."

"Maybe so, but there are two brave men in charge. Sanders and Pyaung will bring it through. All is carefully planned, I assure you. Besides. . . "

"Besides what?"

"There is nothing more either you or I can do, Mr. Fitz. I received the final message from camp last night. They left this morning."

7

THE CARAVAN CREPT along with frequent stops and starts, leaving behind the chaotic, barren cliffs surrounding the camp for the forest belt thick with oak and pine, where an occasional teak with its gray bark and long tobaccolike leaves had managed to survive rapacious logging and where large patches of clearing, covered only with grass, fern, and dwarf bamboo, attested to the passage of poppy farmers, burning and sterilizing the soil within a few seasons, inhibiting the growth of loftier vegetation for years to come.

For centuries, the limpid skies of the Shan States had looked down on similar processions of bony mules, nimble as chamois, panting under loads of contraband, mostly opium, threading their way along unmapped trails where Burma's tiny police force would never dare set foot. But not until now had those skies witnessed such a valuable cargo embarked on a month-long journey over such an extraordinary route. It seemed as if concern for this priceless treasure had filtered down to the humblest members of the expedition who were risking their lives for meager pay: escort soldiers, muleteers, and guides abstained from their usual songs and lively banter. An instinctive, churchlike silence reigned, unbroken but for sporadic, raucous shouts of encouragement to a stumbling mule or the rumble of water signaling a torrent at the foot of an adjacent gorge.

The journey began with a long downhill march in an approximate southwesterly direction toward the Salween. But a column of 120 mules in the highlands is obliged to wind its way, and the half-mile descent through mountain passes and along hairpin turns left the travelers with the impression, at times, of moving backwards. The embryonic trail was apt to disappear or to branch out at several angles, and only the guides knew where to go.

An infantry unit led the march; each soldier with his rifle at the ready, two grenades stuck in his belt, several rations of rice rolled in his pack, wearing a pair of sandals consisting of a meshwork of rubber thongs that would have tripped any Westerner promptly but which had long proved to be the most practical footwear for Shan hill tribesmen, leaving their bare toes free to grip the rocks. Mu, the prince's adjutant, commanded this vanguard. Then came Pyaung himself with a handful of soldiers comprising his bodyguard. He and Sanders were the only two on horseback, riding small mounts no higher than mules—but stockier, nearly as agile over rocky terrain and swifter on level ground.

Next came the mule train, either in single file, or depending on the topography, in a straggling column strung out a mile or more when rugged obstacles along the pathway were long and difficult to negotiate. Then the animals would brace themselves, their backs heaving violently, threatening to burst the pack straps. At such times Butler himself was in agony and felt his muscles straining and contracting in the same manner.

Once a mule got past the hazardous spot with its pack intact—as most did, for the harnesses were securely fastened—and felt solid ground underfoot, it scrambled ahead to catch up. Butler breathed easier and his face relaxed. Not for long, however, because the same ordeal confronted the next mule in line. At such times, the convoy stretched out like an elastic band. Butler would stand rooted on the spot until the last animal had cleared the obstacle. Then, either far below at the foot of a ravine, or high overhead pinpointed against the sky, he could distinguish the lead animals weaving in and out at sharp angles along the mountainside, so remote at times that they seemed part of a different caravan.

Sanders usually rode alongside Pyaung, behind the vanguard, and halted occasionally to inspect the column as it passed. Sometimes he rode with the rear guard. When the footing grew hazardous, he invariably fell in beside Butler.

"Why the devil do you dawdle and lag behind?" he scolded. "There's nothing you can do to help. They have to take care of themselves, and the boys are managing fine without you."

He referred to the muleteers, mountain-bred peasants who walked alongside the animals, calling out to them in flinty language when they needed urging. Now and then, three or four mule drivers would hoist the animals up, one after the other, lifting the saddle packs to lighten the load, sometimes carrying both the beast and its burden.

"What about you?" Butler countered.

"I'm here to keep an eye on the sacks and see that everything goes smoothly. That's my job."

"I'd rather look after things, too. It makes me feel better."

Sanders shrugged his shoulders without getting angry. Since the evening they had planned the expedition, he had been vaguely aware of some mysterious change in this peculiar fellow, once contemptible, now accepted on the merit of his industry, though with little to recommend him

143

for an adventure of this caliber. If the sergeant had written him off initially as a dead loss, he wasn't so sure of it any longer—being a sufficiently good judge of character to realize that Butler's new attitude, his determination to shoulder responsibility, was not sheer bravado. But having little or no training in psychology, he couldn't figure out what was causing a change that perplexed him more and more each day. Several factors were currently prompting him to revert to his original estimate.

He couldn't resist confiding his bewilderment to Prince Pyaung on one of the rare stretches of trail wide enough to accommodate two riders abreast—so puzzled was he by some of the former serviceman's reactions. As they talked, both men eyed the surrounding cliffs for signs of danger.

"Do you know what he asked me the day before we left? I refused him right away and got mad—a gun! And not just any old gun but one of our best, an M-16 carbine. We don't have enough of them to start with."

"One more man with a gun is no hardship," the prince commented, "provided he knows how to use it."

"He does. He showed me."

"And is not *afraid* to use it," Pyaung added solemnly.

"That's exactly what made me hesitate. A gun in the hands of a fellow too scared to fire is. . . "

"Do you think he would be too scared?"

"I don't know what to think anymore," Sanders burst out. "The guy has me completely baffled. I never met any one like him. I told you once how he threw down his gun and ran on the brink of our first action. Not only that, but he refused to fight and abandoned a whole convoy of arms and ammunition we were there to protect. I saw it with my own eyes. And now he begs me to let him have one of our best carbines."

144

"You finally did, I notice," Pyaung observed, casting a furtive glance at the tail of the column.

"Yes, dammit, I did. Something about his manner made me give in. Now I have guilty feelings about it. Do you think I did the wrong thing?"

The Burmese prince paused before answering. The path narrowed, squeezing the two riders into single file. After Sanders took the lead, Pyaung turned around once more. The mules were filed along in close order. He could see Butler in profile, erect against the mountainside, near the middle of the column, hovering over the animals that carried the choicest powder—that which was ninety-eight percent pure. He sat swung around in his saddle for a while, letting the horse have its head. "It's a risk," he said at last, "but I think I would have done the same. Time and circumstances change people. I've known it to happen."

"But don't think I gave in immediately," Sanders protested, flying to his own defense. "I refused and told him straight to his face..."

He went on to relate the whole dialogue, the climax of which had left him more startled than ever. He told Butler frankly that he would never entrust a valuable weapon to a drug addict who might do all sorts of crazy things under the influence of that poisonous stuff, or suffer convulsions as heroin users often do. "'Look at my hands,' he told me, 'they don't tremble'. And it was true, Prince Pyaung, I swear it. Then he said, 'For the last week I haven't taken my morning needle. I've cut my daily dose almost in half. I use it only at night to help me sleep. And I don't get that panicky feeling either. Don't you believe me?...' How could I help but believe him, Prince?" Sanders went on excitedly. "There he stood, just as alert as you see him now on his mule. Not the slightest tremor, just like you or me, the image of determination. But wait, I was not about to swallow a tall tale and I said to him, 'All right, I believe you, but I've known other addicts. Their word isn't worth a nickel. Do you think you can go on this way? How do you know you won't weaken?' Well, you'll never guess what he answered."

The prince had to wait before learning Butler's reply as the rugged terrain kept them advancing Indian file and concentrating on each step the horses took. When they were able to ride side by side again, neither had lost track of the story.

"He said to me, 'Here's my provision for the trip, Sanders.' And he handed me a number of little packets each containing a single dose. He swore that was all he had and turned the whole lot over to me. I'm supposed to give him a packet every night."

"He did that?"

"Yes, he did. That was when I agreed to let him have a carbine. He's kept his word since we left. I give him one packet every night. He takes a single injection. Do you think he could be on the road to recovery after telling me himself that he already went through two cures that didn't work?"

"I read once in the newspapers," Pyaung said, "that Western doctors are trying to cure addicts by moving them to another place, changing their environment. I think they organize round-the-world cruises in France. Maybe a trip on muleback over our trails is one cure your doctors haven't yet thought of."

"Maybe," Sanders murmured dreamily.

"And maybe he is discovering a new interest in life which he never thought was possible."

Sanders looked behind him in turn, sweeping his eyes over the entire caravan, then responded to the prince's smile with a shrug of his shoulders.

8

FITZ RETURNED TO New York two days after his talk with Wong, generally pleased with his trip but prey to anxieties that would well up whenever he thought of the enormous gamble he was taking. Partly in the hope of finding reassurance, he called Herrick into his office to talk about the affair in progress.

"They're on their way. Left six days ago. They've reached the valley of the Salween and are marching southward. Here's where they are, see? Right here."

"The contest is on," said Herrick, "now we have to win it."

"I was right about Wong; he's reliable and shrewd. If the others get to the coast, we'll have won."

"If they get to the coast," Herrick repeated.

"They're getting closer every day. See, here's where they are."

The atlas lay open to a map of Burma on which Fitz had charted the caravan's route. The narrow line began at a point south of Kunlong—in a region tinted dark brown to indicate altitudes 6,000 feet and over—approached the Salween, traversed the Shan States from north to south, crossed Tenasserim, hugged the Thai border close to the river, and ended where the Salween joins one of its tributaries just above the plain of Moulmein.

A bolder line roughly indicated the journey already covered, according to coded information transmitted nightly by Wong, who, at his desk in Rangoon, also monitored the march on a map, but was far too cautious to leave any markings and relied instead on his excellent eyesight and memory.

Herrick, in turn, peered at the outlines of this unfamiliar land. Both men gazed dreamily at the map. A pair of gamblers, but used to operating in a different world, they were experiencing the restless uncertainty of the unknown as they stared at bright-colored patches dotted with strange-sounding names. Fitz especially, after spending years assembling his plan, felt like an outsider to this phase of the operation. No longer did it involve wheeling and dealing, exerting influence, buying favors or silence; there was no more opportunity to work out those tricky schemes so dear to his heart. For the next month he would have no control over the hundreds of men and animals transporting his colossal fortune—a treasure currently jolting through hostile mountains under the watchful eyes of Sanders and Pyaung. Out of a sense of helplessness, he clenched his fists.

The conversation was interrupted by the entrance of Briggs, whom Fitz had also summoned. He was the manager of the tire factory, an engineer with several years' experience in the field, who, like Herrick, had thrown in his lot, for better or worse, with Fitz. Right now he was running the plant efficiently while preparing for activities of another sort. The business was operating successfully enough to act as a screen for the clandestine venture.

Fitz shut the atlas as he entered. Briggs didn't need to know what was going on in Burma.

"Are you all set?"

"Everything's ready. For months we've been receiving regular shipments of rubber bales from this one plantation.

No reason for these others to arouse suspicion. They'll be out in the shed where I keep the rubber we use for experimental purposes. Only Summer, the chemical engineer, and I have access to it."

"Are you sure he's reliable?"

Herrick noticed that his boss was asking this question more and more frequently these days, and with mounting wariness.

"As reliable as I am."

Fitz heaved a sigh. The necessity of revealing certain phases of the operation to others tormented him. Briggs had to be in on the secret, and Summer as well. Of course, he had known them a long time and thought they could be trusted—for the same reasons Herrick could be trusted. Still, when you added them to Wong, Sanders, Pyaung, Butler, the manager of the Malayan plantation, and one of his aides, plus at least two more workers and a handful of others, that meant a lot of people—too many to suit him. But what else could he do? It takes brains and brawn to extract, transport, and handle five tons of heroin.

Briggs explained a few other matters and left. Fitz's mood shifted suddenly as he clutched Herrick by the shoulder, hammering out his words with desperate insistence. "It's *got* to work, Herrick. I've poured everything I could into it."

Only then did Herrick sense the anguish behind the impassive mask. The risk still was great, despite all their precautions; the outlay, enormous, but only a drop in the bucket compared to the fruits of success. Yet who could tell what was going on this very moment in the Shan States?

"The crucial thing is for the caravan to reach the coast," Fitz went on in a muffled voice. "Right now they face all sorts of obstacles including rival bands—robbers armed to the teeth who must begin to suspect what's in transit. In less than a week—Wong gave me the approximate

149

schedule—they'll be passing through a region infeste
with them, where the Burmese prince has no influenc
Anything can happen."

"There's not a thing you can do," said Herrick, th
fatalist. "Or I, for that matter."

Those were Wong's own words, words of wisdom. Bu
they merely added fuel to Fitz's uncertainty. Droppin
Herrick's arms, he ran his hand over his forehead as
gripped by a sudden dizzy spell.

"Not a thing, you're right. For a month the whole ver
ture will hang on two men. . . three billion dollars, Herricl
in the hands of an ex-marine sergeant and a Burmes
mercenary."

In his office at the Narcotics Bureau, Stephens also wa
poring over a map of Burma with his aide Allen.

"They left several days ago," said Stephens. "I can'
chart their hourly progress because our agents aren't al
lowed to enter Burma. Besides, I told them not to; there'
no point sounding the alarm. They're waiting in Thailand
collecting whatever information they can. I expect detail
momentarily. Gyi was able to join them."

"Your deaf-mute?"

"Mute, yes, but not deaf, and I hope he's had his ear
open. He made it to Thailand after the caravan left, since h
wasn't going on it. My men are interrogating him right now
I'll have word tomorrow or in the next few days; it take
time to get information out of a mute who doesn't under
stand any civilized tongue. He's clever though, and even i
he can't speak, he can count, draw, and make facial expres
sions. I know already that they're marching south, skirtin
the valley of the Salween."

"General direction—Moulmein," Allen added, glanc
ing at the map.

"Or thereabouts. You can be sure they'll stay clear of the cities. Somewhere on the coast probably, along the Gulf of Martaban, or on the Salween, if not some other river. Junks can penetrate quite far inland. We'll find out. Once it leaves the docks, the shipment shouldn't be hard to trace here. That's not what bothers me."

"I think I know what's upsetting you, sir," said Allen after a moment's pause.

"It's not hard to figure out. In that pirate-infested country, every step they take is a hazard."

The narcotics chief was captive more or less to the same anxiety that was currently plaguing the smugglers: fear for the caravan's safety. He was hoping against hope that the cargo would arrive intact. Informed by his spies, including Gyi the mute, of the presence of unusually large stores of narcotics atop a mountain peak in the Shan States and their seaward transit on muleback, he assumed instantly that they were bound for the United States. Relying on the facts he already knew and the Bureau's resources outside Burma, Stephens felt confident that he could unmask whatever disguise the traffickers would choose to use in the final phase. Hope dawned that he could track the heroin to its destination and thus uncover the organization and the masterminds of this gigantic scheme. To arrest a crew of hirelings in Burma—even if he managed to do it —would serve no purpose. So for several days he lived with the haunting fear that the cargo might get scattered to the four winds, fall into pirate hands and be spread over the globe—dashing his hopes of trapping the real criminals. He vented his distress through frantic agitation not unlike Fitz's behavior.

"God, Allen, I just hope nothing happens to them in that land of savages. Pray that the caravan and its load reaches the sea. If it does, we've won."

9

ATTENDED BY THE desires, the fears, and the hopes of as
sorted gamblers in the East and the West, the caravan crep
deeper, daily, hourly, into the forests dominating the bank
of the Salween. The restless hooves of the mules bore the
treasure along like a giant centipede whose ribs expand an
contract to accommodate the terrain over which it crawls
The river peeked out from time to time through folds in the
landscape and crevices in the forest wall, looking slightl
broader and less crystalline than from the mountai
peaks.

The soldiers had not been called on to use thei
weapons and the prince anticipated no trouble for severa
days to come. Actually, the passage through friendly ham
lets under his sway made it possible to relax more than i
the wilderness during stopovers, and to trade off the tire
mules against fresh ones for a few additional Indian rupees
coins that dated back to the British occupation and whic
Pyaung carried with him. Hill tribes in the Shan State
refused to trade in any other currency.

Headaches they had, but of a different sort. The sk
had clouded over suddenly the night before. Rain pelte
the forest since early morning, slowing the march, crum
bling boulders on the heights, and transforming sand

avines into beds of slippery mud laced with rivulets.

The trail they were now descending seemed endless to
Butler. At the tail of the column, among the infantry rear
guard, he fretted to see the last mules lurching almost every
step of the way. Like everyone else in the caravan, soldiers
and muleteers alike, he wore the traditional umbrella-like
Chinese hat made of straw, coated with shellac, which pro-
tected its wearer from the rain but also curtained him off
behind a moving cascade, nearly opaque in a downpour.
Fortunately, the stores were sheltered; he checked the
packs at each halt. But the prospect of having to cross a
torrent at the bottom of the canyon filled him with dread.
He thought he could already hear the roaring river swollen
by heavy rains.

By standing up in the wire meshwork that served as
stirrups, he could see the successive spans of the caravan
strung out zigzag along the mountainside. The straw hats of
the muleteers, amidst the animals, poked up like giant
orange mushrooms. Daylight was fading as shadows closed
in on the rear section. He heard the roaring—not so imaginary this time—of distant rushing waters.

In the lead, Sanders and Pyaung reached the riverbank,
each haunted by the same apprehension. The prince halted
and had to shout to make himself heard. "Devilish rain!
The stream has doubled in volume and is rising every minute. Unless we cross tonight, we'll never make it. Tomorrow we'll have to take a long detour or else wait for the
waters to recede."

"Wait? How long?" Sanders asked.

"That depends on the rain. If it stops, the level will
drop quickly; otherwise, several days."

"And the detour?"

"Over thirty miles. The same distance back to the main
road."

153

"That's at least three days. Impossible. We'll have t
cross tonight."

The lead mules had come to a halt atop the mudd
bank sloping down to the torrent; immobilized by the sigh
and the din of roaring water, their ears pricked up, rain an
foam dripping from their flanks.

"Is that your decision?"

"It has to be," Sanders declared. "We can't afford sucl
a delay."

"Wait here. I'll see if it can be done."

Tossing aside his nuisance of a straw hat, the prince se
heels to his horse which balked before consenting to de
scend the slippery mud bank. The animal must have bee
used to this type of exercise as it slid down toboggan
fashion on its rump, hind legs bent, rising only to enter th
stream after one last protest. The horse advanced knee
deep into the swirling foam, then up to its belly, and then i
lost its balance and for just a second or two, its frantic hea
alone was visible while Pyaung, three-quarters immersed
remained riveted in the saddle. The horse regained its foot
ing almost instantly and scrambled ashore, snorting an
shaking its coat. The driftage was not too bad, and the fa
slope not too steep. The prince urged his mount back acros
the stream, halting in the water directly below Sanders.

"Easy enough for me," he shouted up. "Risky, but no
impossible, for the loaded mules. If the lead mule follow
me, the rest will fall in. I'll wait on the far bank while the
cross. You wait here. We must hurry; in an hour it will b
too late."

He gave rapid orders to the first muleteer, who bowe
silently. The others understood and, without a murmur o
protest, prepared to move ahead.

The mule driver yanked the bridle of the lead anima

154

urging it forward in a husky bawl while two cohorts pushed from behind. The mule hesitated, then like the horse, slid down the slope straight into the water. The man held fast to the bridle until the mule had waded in up to its belly; then he lost his balance, drifting down toward the tail, reaching out to grab it, shouting all the while in what appeared to be a familiar maneuver. The mule, in turn, lost its footing and began to swim straight for Pyaung's horse, responding to its urgent whinnies. It drifted no more than the horse had off its course and clambered onto solid ground as the next mule repeated the same maneuver.

Sanders and the prince directed the crossing from both sides of the torrent; hastening it whenever possible, for dusk was falling rapidly along with the rain and the river continued to rise slowly and insidiously. The tail end of the caravan had the worst time of it. Some of the men formed a chain to prod the animals—a chain that broke, unfortunately, in the deepest part of the stream.

The mishap involved the last two animals—after everything had gone so well and Sanders was just heaving a sigh of relief. The first of the two mules lost its footing and was carried off by a sudden thrust of the current, escaping the grasp of its driver who floundered ashore. The second animal panicked and tore free of its guide, and the two beasts were swept along, struggling against the current instead of striking out for the opposite bank.

Sanders reacted instantly. He had already rid himself of the hat which had made it difficult to see, and unbuckled his belt. In a flash he ripped off the belt, dropped his gun, leaped off his horse and rushed into the stream. Seizing the mule by its bridle, he turned its head toward the far bank in an effort to co-ordinate the animal's frantic churning. The mule recovered its footing after both man and beast had

155

been swept along for some thirty yards. Intending to aban
don the still trembling animal, he turned—about to plunge
toward the second one, when he saw that it had already
been guided out of the water and was climbing up the bank
further downstream. Its rescuer gripped the bridle firmly.

It was Butler. Quick reflexes, almost as quick as mine
Sanders thought, with a trace of contempt. Did he copy me
or did he act instinctively at the same time I did? The
sergeant pondered this—a rather absurd question at a time
when other matters demanded his attention. The agitated
mules had to be quieted and the caravan reorganized; yet
this one point so preoccupied him that he thought of noth
ing else the whole time he was restoring the column to
order.

The soldiers crossed safely, gripping a rope slung across the
stream. By nightfall the operation was over. Both men and
beasts needed to rest. Pyaung called a halt on a grassy knoll
where the mules were unsaddled and left to graze and to
calm themselves. Sentinels took their posts. The prince
gave permission for fires to be lit so that the men could dry
off and cook their rice; then they stretched out on the
ground wrapped in half-damp blankets.

The moment they halted, even before removing his
drenched clothing, Sanders had brought out a flask of whis
key and poured a stiff drink for each of his companions and
himself. He and the Burmese prince stared at Butler as they
gulped it down, their mute attention conveying more than
words. Butler, who was ordinarily a temperate drinker
emptied his cup slowly and with relish, savoring every
drop. When he had finished, his eyes blazed with a flame no
drug had ever kindled. The trio put on fresh, relatively dry

clothes, and not a word was said about the incident before they ate.

After supper, Butler pleaded weariness and retired to his sleeping bag. He had unrolled it at some distance from the two leaders, close to the saddle packs containing the precious powder that stood in the center of the camp. Pyaung and Sanders exchanged further glances and poured themselves one last drink.

"Apparently, he trusts no one but himself to guard the treasure," Sanders observed.

The prince nodded his head. "And once in a while he seems to be right. But for him and you, we would have lost. . ."

Sanders injected a question that had been bothering him since the crossing. "I did the normal thing. That's what I'm here for. But what I want to know is whether he followed me or jumped in at the same time."

"At the same time. . ."

Sanders rapped his forehead and interrupted again. "What a fool I am! He probably was too shy to ask for it. I forgot to give him his evening dose. I don't want to encourage his habit, but today of all days he certainly deserves it."

Rummaging in his gear, he brought out one of the packets and took it over to Butler. He returned a few moments later, looking very puzzled, which prompted a quizzical glance from Pyaung.

"Do you know what he said when I handed him the drug? Calm as you please: 'Thanks, not tonight; tomorrow will do.' The fellow never ceases to amaze me."

Pyaung probably shared his surprise but never revealed such reactions. "A day that ends well for everyone," was all he said. "For the caravan, a perilous obstacle safely behind; for him. . . "

157

"For him also; I see what you mean. Still, for my own peace of mind, I'd like to see him trapped in an ambush now, like in the old days, under fire, fighting for his life."

"Don't wish any such thing," Pyaung warned, "the journey isn't over."

After a pause, the prince revived the subject they had been discussing earlier. "He jumped in at the same time you did. Without you two, we would have lost 250 pounds of merchandise, not to mention two mules. I marveled at your quick reactions."

Rarely did the prince hand out compliments. The episode truly must have impressed him. The two men burrowed into their sleeping bags. The rain had stopped, promise of a restful night. Stars began to peek through the clouds. Sanders felt he should return the compliment.

"Well, I liked the way you plunged right into the stream before you even knew how deep it was."

"But I didn't share your impulse to leap off my horse and into the torrent," said the prince with an odd smile.

"We must have acted only seconds before you. I'm sure you were about to."

"Not on your life," Pyaung objected, grinning broadly, and snuggling down deeper under the covers. "I'll tell you a secret: I can't swim."

10

ALLEN ENTERED STEPHENS'S office feeling highly optimistic, with every reason to expect a pat on the back. But when he found his boss wearing a long face, he waited to hear the cause of it before presenting his report.

"Things gone wrong out there, sir?"

Stephens shrugged his shoulders in silent rage and raised his scowling face. His aide had found him hunched over the map of Burma, a recent habit of his. This affair meant more to him than anything else at the moment, now that he knew what was at stake, and some other matters were being neglected as a result.

"Bunglers! They've lost four mules and their packs on the southern Sino-Burma road. They should have known better than to take that road in the first place."

"Four? There still must be plenty left."

"A hundred and sixteen."

"I see you're better informed about the situation now, sir."

"Yes, a little. I know this isn't a fatal tragedy, but a few more such mishaps will really mess things up for us. They're not even halfway there."

"Ambushed? By the Lahus—the ones you were worried about?"

"No, they haven't even reached the real danger zone They ran into a so-called government patrol—whatever tha means out there. Their rear guard was fired at and fou mules either hit, or so badly frightened, that they rushe pell-mell over the brink of a gorge. They thought it was . full-scale attack, which it wasn't. With just a little effort the could have won out and recovered the goods."

"It wouldn't exactly do for us to assign then bodyguards. . ." Allen's comment died under a witherin look from his chief who was in no mood for jokes.

"In any event, they chose to save their skins and get ou with the bulk of the caravan intact. The patrol was afraid t pursue them in the dark—besides, they already had thei booty, a real windfall. Imagine, over 400 pounds of choic heroin! And what did those members of God-knows-wha national militia do? They deserted on the spot and dashe off to sell their plunder to Thai dealers, boasting about th exploit. That's how my agents obtained such precise de tails."

"And valuable too."

"Yes. . . a curious thing, Allen, apart from the inciden itself: my people got their hands on a sample of the loot an sent it over here immediately. I had Bridget analyze it—yo know, that crazy girl who did us such a great service!"

"What's happened to her since her boyfriend disap peared?"

"Nothing very cheerful. She's pining away, sees n one, and seems to have lost her zest for work. I heard she' been absent a lot from the laboratory and they're not ver pleased with her. Anyway, I don't give a damn. She can g to the devil! But at least she or her assistants can still tur out an accurate analysis—and apparently that's what rouse her from her torpor, what jolted her out of her rut. Do yo know why? Can you guess the results she phoned in, begging to know where we had made the seizure, information that's none of her business, and which, of course, I didn't give her. Well, it was ninety-six percent, Allen, ninety-six percent pure heroin!"

"Even better than. . ."

"That's right—even better than that Indiana batch, the one we believe was turned out by that confounded addict who vanished without a trace."

"You suspect Butler?"

"I'm always suspicious when these coincidences crop up. And I'll find out for certain. Look, I now have a full report from the mute helper—who's no deafer than you are—in that blasted laboratory perched like an eagle's nest. . . I say report, though God knows my men had some job interrogating a mute who can't even write his name; it's a real thriller. Anyway, they found out a good deal. Thanks to this Gyi, I now know the weight of the heroin. He used to have to set it on the scales. Five tons, Allen—a fortune! It's incredible. I also know that there were 120 mules in the original train, 116 today, headed for the coast of Tenasserim, just as I thought. Thank God the fellow can draw! My people kept after him for three days and finally came up with a description of the principals in the camp who are now with the caravan. There are three of them, Allen: one is a Burmese hill chief they call 'prince', who wears his hair long and provides soldiers. I don't care about him—his own blasted government can worry about stringing him up. The second man is white, a hard drinker, and sounds just like a former marine sergeant I heard about in Thailand, another soldier of fortune. The third, Allen, is the chemist who made those five tons of heroin worth billions of dollars over here. I've figured it out; you won't believe it, but there's enough to poison over half the States for a year! Here's a description of the chemist—better still, a composite sketch of him based on Gyi's impressions. Look at it."

Allen read the description and gazed at the sketch. "I've never laid eyes on Butler," he said at last, "but from what my agents tell me, it looks just like him. May I show them the picture?"

"Go ahead; I've got other copies. I'll show it to Edmund, too, since he knew him personally. Maybe Bridget as well, but even if she recognized it she wouldn't say so. I want positive identification, though I'm confident it's he."

"So am I, sir, and for another reason, too."

"Really?"

"With your permission, I pressed our Indiana inquiry as far as I could and I think it turned up the first solid clue."

Stephens prodded him impatiently. "For heaven's sake, what is it, Allen? Tell me."

"It has to do with Fitz, sir. I've learned something new about him. It turns out that he and Herrick are in touch —and that's not all."

The Bureau's constant surveillance of Herrick over the years had provided a record of the persons he saw from time to time. Each of them was investigated—thus far with no results. That was how the Bureau had first heard of Fitz. His reputation as a successful businessman seemed to place him above suspicion, but Stephens, acting on a hunch, had ordered his agents to pursue the matter further.

"You know that our people in Indiana finally located the laboratory, though it had been dismantled and the couple running the ranch had gone away without leaving an address. Still, certain signs are very clear."

"I know all that. So?"

"Well, I hired professionals to sift through the records of land-title offices throughout the county. Tedious job and very confusing, but it was fruitful in the end. The ranch owner vanished also, but Fitz turns out to be the person who put up the deposit money at the time of purchase, years ago."

Stephens stiffened and took a deep, rasping breath, his nostrils dilating like a gun dog coming to the point. "Nice work, Allen. Herrick, Butler; Herrick, Fitz; the laboratory. My hunch was right. Butler was out there working for Fitz and he still is in Burma."

"All the more," Allen added nonchalantly, "since Fitz made a recent trip to the Far East and spent several days in Burma."

Stephens took a second deep breath, paused, and commented, "I see you've done your homework, too."

"He had a girl with him, a dancer, very pretty, the type he goes for; dumped her when he got back. Knowing your interest in him, I put an agent—a handsome fellow—onto her. That way I learned a few things. Oh, nothing really sensational or suspicious. He goes on a pleasure trip of this sort each year. Took in the sights in every country he visited. I also know that in Rangoon he left his girlfriend alone for most of one afternoon instead of taking his usual nap. On the day the caravan left, according to what you told me, sir."

"Good work, Allen," said Stephens, rubbing his hands together. "The pieces are beginning to fit together."

"There's something else; at least I think so, sir. I kept the best news for last."

Beneath his chief's probing stare, Allen dropped his voice, speaking in hushed, solemn tones. "A little over a year ago, a certain tire factory in New York State changed hands. It was bought by a new group, cheaply, too, because the business was going downhill. It revived quickly under

163

dynamic management and with new capital. Well, on th
list of its board of directors, I once again discovered th
name of Fitz."

This time Stephens emitted a long, low whistle—
habit of his when he felt excited and confident that he wa
on the right track. He eyed his aide with fresh admiration
"I presume you didn't just happen to stumble on that piec
of information."

"Not exactly, sir. As a matter of fact, I was followin;
two different tracks that finally converged."

"At Fitz?"

"At Fitz. On the one hand, I began to sort through al
his business connections—and God knows there ar
plenty—all honest for the most part, I'm now convinced. O
the other hand, in one of our recent talks I got th
impression. . ."

In recent weeks, after pooling all the information a
hand, Stephens had begun to see what the organization an
the man running it were up to: by lying low for a while
they hoped to throw their chief foe, the Bureau, off th
scent, while they prepared for a great splash, a single hau
big enough to set up every last one of the gangsters for life
He was practically certain that one enormous shipment o
drugs, labeled as some other product, would arrive by boat
And so, with the same meticulous care typical of Wong, th
Chinese, he began to scrutinize lists of cargo dispatched t
the United States from Burmese and other Southeast Asian
ports. (He knew that black marketeers of this calibe
wouldn't hesitate to arrange one or more transfers to cove
the trail.) Also like Wong, he adopted certain logica
guidelines: the merchandise had to be ordinary, abundant
and heavy. Again like Wong, he boiled a great many choice
down to one or two possibilities. Rubber headed his shor
list.

164

Stephens recalled having mentioned all this to Allen one day, only casually, because his findings were purely speculative and therefore to be taken with a grain of salt. Apparently, however, the words had not fallen on deaf ears, and right now he felt pleased with himself for hiring such an alert assistant. Casting the young man a thankful look, he murmured, "Rubber, Allen," with a slight tremor in his voice.

"Rubber, sir. For the past year, this factory has been receiving a large monthly shipment of rubber bales from a plantation in northern Malaya, not far from Penang."

11

THE CARAVAN LEFT the Shan States and entered Tenasserim, having covered over half the journey with no mishap worse than the loss of four mules and their packs. The column marched on toward the coast, undaunted by such ordinary obstacles as another broad, deep tributary of the Salween to cross. The mules were unsaddled and made to swim while soldiers carried the goods across a shaky bridge of plaited vines. Neither were they unnerved by an encounter with a local bandit chief, who, with his armed followers, appeared to talk things over, he said. Pyaung knew him and had already paid him off, but the chief, after seeing the size of the caravan, had changed his mind and raised the price. Though the visible raiding party was small, the prince's practiced eye detected suspicious stirrings among the rocks overhead. Prudent as he was brave, he conferred with Sanders and with Butler, whose suggestions he now accepted. After putting their heads together, they decided to pay the not-so-exorbitant surcharge. Settlement was made, as usual, in silver rupees. The pirate leader declared his satisfaction and rode off with his band.

The Salween was nearing Thailand. The column plunged into the mountains flanking the ill-defined frontier between the two countries. On the Thai side, at a healthy distance, agents of the Narcotics Bureau managed to follow the caravan's progress through lookouts posted on peaks reached by trails too narrow for mules.

The timing of the Lahu ambush testified to the hostile tribesmen's knowledge of the caravan's itinerary and make-up. It broke out during the ascent of a mile-high ridge overlooked by even higher crests. A narrow path hewn out of the rock provided the only access for mules.

This steeply rising defile, squeezed between the cliff on one side and a gully on the other, spelled trouble to Pyaung who ordered a halt while scouts went ahead, his usual strategy in hazardous corridors. A burst of gunfire greeted the scouting party. The pass was guarded, by Lahus no doubt, who considered it their turf. There was no room for bargaining. The muleteers flattened the animals against the cliff and tried to calm those frightened by the shooting. The soldiers crouched down among the rocks and aimed sporadic volleys, more or less haphazardly, in the direction of their unseen foes.

The caravan had to get through; it was the only route. Leaving a handful of men with Sanders, Pyaung took the bulk of his troops and began to scale the cliff from another point off the pathway, planning to reach the summit and attack the pirates from behind.

Sanders, at the head of the stationary convoy, looked sullen. Instinct and combat experience made him frown on such tactics, though he said nothing. Memories of Korea and Vietnam hinted of a trap. The gunfire from the pass was not very brisk; it could be a diversion to cover up the main attack. At the first shots, he leaped off his horse and stood listening, one finger on the trigger of his carbine.

When the prince and his men had gone, he left his

horse with a muleteer and walked to the rear of the convoy, taking with him most of the soldiers nearby. Halfway down the line, he met Butler, who, equally confused, was hurrying backward along the corridor. At that moment, the main attack broke out.

It started when a mine exploded on the path close to the two Americans, and carved a yawning breach that split the column into two isolated segments. Simultaneously, a burst of gunfire rang out from the heights. Bewildered at first, Sanders managed to get hold of himself and cursed roundly. A bullet had struck him in the thigh. Clutching his wound, he dragged himself behind a rock to regain his composure and size up the situation. The enemy's tactics were perfectly predictable: while fire from above pinned the soldiers to the ledge, a raiding party was swooping down the mountain to seize the segment of the caravan that had been cut off by the mine explosion. The rear guard, which was small and stunned by the avalanche tumbling down from the sky, offered faint resistance. The handful of men with Sanders couldn't skirt the breach without drawing fire from hidden foes. The mule drivers had stretched themselves out against the side of the cliff. Even now Lahus were grabbing mules by their bridles, turning them around and urging them back down the path where a few had fled in blind panic after the explosion. Half the mule train was galloping off.

Tears of rage welled up in Sanders's eyes. Most of the Shan soldiers were way up ahead with the prince. Half the treasure was disappearing as the bandits dragged, prodded, and excited the mules. Though wounded, he kept on firing, cursing, and yelling orders at the pocket of soldiers presumably behind him.

"We've got to stop them," he shouted, "we've got to run them down."

But nothing was happening. Were the soldiers refusing to obey him now that their familiar leader was gone? Darting a desperate glance behind him, he found himself alone. "Good God! They've run! Where's Butler?"

Butler, he just remembered, had been nearby at the time of the explosion. He, too, had disappeared; the spot where he had been standing was deserted. This so enraged Sanders that he forgot his own peril and began cursing afresh. "Damn bastard! Turned tail again and the others followed. I might have expected it. I never should have let him come along. Chicken once, chicken always. I'll fix his hash for good if I ever get out of here!"

The fusillade was dying out. In no time the bandits up on the peak would be withdrawing. Sanders struggled desperately to get to his feet, but fell back with a cry of pain. All he could do was wait for Pyaung to return with the bulk of the troops; too late, alas, to catch the thieves. Half the cargo was gone, vanished from sight. He began to cry like a baby.

At last he saw some men from the vanguard approaching, led by Mu, the Burmese prince's adjutant. He didn't have time to wonder why Pyaung hadn't plunged straight into the fray at the outset. Instinctively, he moved toward them, and a bolt of pain shot through his thigh. His eyes clouded over as he fell back unconscious.

He never heard the new burst of gunfire from below —at the point where the path, after twisting in and out, disappeared into the forest.

Night was falling when he regained consciousness. Bewildered, he found himself lying on a stretcher carried by two soldiers. His thigh, swathed in a crude bandage, was throbbing. The caravan was descending a moderately gentle slope. He tried to speak and could barely hear the sound of his own voice. He must have lost a lot of blood. Behind him, one of the soldiers shouted a warning. Someone came riding up along the path, weaving past several mules, and approached him. It was Butler.

Sanders, suddenly remembering the whole episode, clenched his fists but felt too weak to vent his anger.

"How do you feel?"

"Not as chipper as you do, I'll bet," the sergeant answered scornfully.

Butler seemed taken aback and changed the subject. "We came through the pass quite a while ago. I think we're about ready to camp for the night. I'll look after you. They made you a temporary bandage to stop the bleeding; we had to clear out of there as fast as we could. I ordered the column to move on."

"*You*... gave the orders?" Sanders wavered between indignation and stupefaction.

Butler spoke like a leader and went on to speak forcefully. "There was no choice. We were sitting ducks at the foot of those cliffs and the bandits might have returned in force. Now we're on better ground; we'll camp here tonight."

He cupped his hands to his mouth and trumpeted the Shan signal to halt. Muleteers passed the command down the line, which stood still. The two stretcher-bearers set down their load and mopped their brows.

"Excuse me," Butler said in the same authoritative manner, "I have to give the orders for pitching camp and for sentry duty. I'll tell you the whole story later, if you're interested. Right now, try to rest."

He had already mounted his mule and was about to ride past the column when Sanders flung one last, implor-

170

ing, question at him. "Just tell me this: the mules, what happened to the ones in the rear?"

"We lost five," Butler replied curtly. "I couldn't help it. But I got all the others back."

Digging his heels into the mule, he disappeared up the line, leaving Sanders hopelessly bewildered—groping in a fog that his fever only aggravated. Of all the questions plaguing him, one emerged as paramount. Now that he, Sanders, was disabled, it wasn't up to Butler to issue orders as he was doing, especially in regard to pitching camp. The sergeant had picked up a few Shan phrases and tried to interrogate one of his bearers. "Where's the prince?"

"Dead," the man answered, dropping his eyes. He pointed behind the stretcher.

Slowly, painfully, Sanders twisted his head around and saw Pyaung's horse in back of him. Across the saddle, framed by two bodyguards, lay the Burmese prince's body, his long hair sweeping the ground.

Sanders had no chance to react or to wonder what had caused this death or his own injury. The mules were advancing again; moving off the trail into the forest, heading for a certain spot designated by an authority. "He gave orders, he's the one giving orders," he kept mumbling as the fever mounted. "My God, what'll happen to us in the hands of that blasted junkie?"

12

JUST AS HE had said, Butler immediately took charge of pitching camp, using as an interpreter the prince's adjutant who spoke a few garbled words of English. At first Mu hesitated to obey, then bowed and transmitted the orders. The mules were unsaddled and tethered beneath the trees, the stores deposited in a central place under double guard. Then there were the casualties to look after. Five dead soldiers and a muleteer had been left behind. Only the body of Pyaung had been carried there by his personal bodyguards who were preparing to bury it. Minor injuries were treated by orderlies with basic nursing skills. Eight critically injured men lay moaning on the ground. What to do with them would be decided before breaking camp the next morning.

Only after settling these matters did Butler return to Sanders, whom the bearers had transferred onto his sleeping bag. Aided by an orderly, he cleaned the wound and rebandaged it. The sergeant himself, who was used to such things, examined his thigh and instructed the attendants. "It shouldn't be too bad unless it gets infected," he growled. "But I won't be able to walk or ride a horse for two weeks."

"We'll carry you. In ten days the trip will be over."

Sanders nodded glumly. "In the meantime, do you expect these boys to act like sheep under your command? I admit you're doing all right for the moment, but wait a bit. . . Say, when are you going to tell me what happened back there? I folded up just as those damn robbers were dragging off half the pack train."

The explosion and the opening hail of gunfire had left Butler immobilized, panic-stricken, just as the threat of danger had affected him in Vietnam. But the initial shock didn't last. A feeling stronger than fear had prevailed: the compelling necessity to deal swiftly with a critical problem which claimed all his mental resources and ruled out any trembling of his limbs. He tried to explain his state of mind without either inflating or deflating his actions. "Listen, when I saw them dashing for the mules, I saw total disaster in store. We were cut off from them by a chasm, and the people above kept us from skirting it. Over two tons of my heroin vanished right before my eyes."

"Don't you think I know it?"

"Including the most valuable sacks with my latest, choicest batch."

"Can't say I was in any shape to notice that," Sanders growled.

"You were still stunned by the explosion when I leaped."

"You leaped?"

"Over the edge, or just about. I had to do something instantly, you know. Pyaung and his men would have come back too late. As for trying to circuit the breach, we would have been picked off one by one. Suddenly I realized what we had to do. I don't mean I *thought* it; I *felt* it, actually, like an electric shock. I was propelled by an irresistible force."

He relived the instant with frantic intensity bordering on hallucination, as if it marked a decisive turning point in his life, as if he couldn't bear to forget a single image or sensation of the whole staggering experience. He talked with feverish excitement, anxious to communicate, to re-create, the whirlwind that had swept him off his feet, and now and then his tone took on the triumphant ring that Sanders knew so well: the sound of his own voice narrating past exploits to Pyaung.

"I signaled to the soldiers near us. They kept holding back; a sign wasn't enough. So I grabbed one by the shoulders and leaped—yes, leaped—both of us went sliding down perpendicular to the path. The men on the peak couldn't see us any more. Do you follow me?"

"Sure. But it was like a precipice, wasn't it?"

"Almost. Rocks were crumbling under us, but I held fast to the soldier and my carbine. The others caught on and followed. Brave men, they simply needed to be shown the way. All of us rolled down in a shower of flying rubble —clutching our rifles—to where the winding path reappeared below. I didn't stop there; we had to go on. So I plunged off again, dragging the others with me, just in time to see the first mule arriving untended on the path. But we had to get still farther away from the peak, and down we went, straight down. The mules took the same trail they had come on; they had no choice. Down we rolled, past a second, a third, a fourth bend, straight down. I've got black-and-blue marks and bruises all over me, nothing serious. We wound up nearly on the floor of the ravine. I left my men there, hidden in the forest."

"*Your* men! You're starting to sound like a marine sergeant," Sanders growled.

"Then it was our turn to set a trap with the terrain and

the element of surprise in our favor. And they no longer were covered from above. See my plan?"

"Do I!" exclaimed Sanders, so engrossed in the scene now that he forgot the pain in his thigh. "Pretty neat for a junkie, under fire at that. . . . Listen, Butler," and here his voice changed, "I have to tell you something: I was sure you'd turned tail. I called you a coward. I owe you an apology. I swore I'd kill you if I ever laid eyes on you."

Butler shrugged his shoulders as if to dismiss the matter and went on with his story. The rest was easy to guess. Before long, the bandits appeared with the stolen mules. To avoid any mishap, he ordered his men to hold fire until they were at close range. They fired point-blank, mowing down the raiders and sending them into a panic. The survivors thought they were outnumbered and took to their heels, abandoning their plunder except for five mules which had galloped down toward the foot of the ravine.

"I wanted to chase the thieves but there were too few of us. At some point they would have realized that. Out in the open, we didn't stand a chance. Besides, we had to round up the mules who were dashing all over the place, and get back up the cliff to find out what was happening on top. I decided to cut our losses."

"You were right," Sanders nodded, "there are times when you can't afford any more losses." He made a quick mental calculation. "Five plus four, that's nine animals gone, just over 1,000 pounds, say ten percent. That's a normal loss for this type of operation and I'm sure the higher-ups figured on it. But it leaves no margin and the trip isn't over yet."

"Pyaung warned us that that was the worst lap. That's why I gave orders to march at once. In ten days we'll be there."

"If all goes well. We've lost Pyaung," Sanders noted grimly, "a valuable man, and a friend besides. With him along, we knew we could rely on the soldiers. Now. . ."

The sentence trailed off. He knew that Shan soldiers would have followed their leader to the end of the earth. With Pyaung gone and the day marked by heavy losses, the men were bound to make trouble.

"They obeyed me," Butler declared. "With you injured and the prince dead, I felt I had to take charge immediately, before they had a chance to think about it. They obeyed me and they'll continue to obey," he repeated emphatically.

Sanders stared hard at him, more and more mystified, now with a glimmer of respect. "A talent for leadership," he muttered, "never would have dreamed it. Anyway, you did the right thing. They followed you because they were in imminent danger; also because your conduct—and by that I mean your plunge over the edge—impressed them. You can be sure that right now the ones who went with you are telling the others how decisively you acted. A great plus in your favor. The problem is that once the danger's past and they start thinking about it, tonight or tomorrow, no one knows what they'll do."

"They'll march where they're told to," Butler asserted, smiling. "I guarantee it."

Sanders stared at him in silence. "You'll ride my horse," he said at last. "It's important to these men. As for me, I can only help you with advice—if you need it," he added with an unfamiliar touch of humility.

"All right. Now try to sleep."

"Not before I inform Wong. I want to do it myself."

Sanders had the radio transmitter brought to him, along with paper and pencil. Butler left to inspect the camp and make sure that the sentinels were on duty.

The sergeant watched him walk away, then shook his

head as if to dispel the cloud of confusion in his mind. He began composing his message, which he sent, slowly, and with difficulty, over the transmitter. He knew that Wong listened at the same hour each evening. In less than fifteen minutes, the reply came back. Wong had a flair for sizing up critical situations and making rapid decisions. Pending consultation with the higher-ups, he took it upon himself to confirm Butler's command of the expedition, as Sanders proposed.

Butler was slow in returning. The injured sergeant felt his fever soaring and couldn't sleep. He kept thinking of all the troubles they were bound to have with the prince gone, and he tossed and turned and cursed his helpless condition.

He heard shouts from the center of the camp, then Butler's voice rising imperiously, dominating the others. He seemed angry and was speaking English; it sounded as if Mu was translating his words. Butler reappeared shortly, accompanied by the adjutant and two soldiers with scowling faces. Mu himself looked grim. The sergeant gathered that their troubles had started.

"Tell them to lay down their arms," Butler ordered the interpreter. "Tomorrow, they will replace two of the muleteers."

A humiliating punishment. Mu glanced at Sanders who nodded for him to obey. He did, grudgingly, and translated the command into the Shan tongue which is like no other. Reluctantly, the two soldiers laid down their rifles.

"They can't have them back until I think they've been sufficiently disciplined. Now tell them to get out of my sight."

"What did they do?" Sanders asked after the pair had left.

"I forbade any fires tonight. This is still a danger zone. They disobeyed my order."

Sanders knew the gravity of the offense, and, despite his raging fever, mustered every syllable of Shan at his command and every ounce of authority over these hill people among whom he had lived for so long, in order to defend Butler against Mu. "Prince Pyaung would have punished them more severely, you know."

"Mu knows this; but he was Prince Pyaung."

"He's dead now and I'm in no condition to take command. Someone has to do it if we're going to get out of here. The great chief to whom I telegraphed has designated this man. The soldiers must obey him, just as I will."

It was a rather unscrupulous ploy, Sanders knew, but highly expedient. Actually, he had radio contact only with Wong in Rangoon, whose rank in the organization was little higher than his own. But sometime before, a rumor had started among the soldiers that the sergeant conferred each evening with a very important and mysterious personage—a rumor which he did nothing to discourage, and, in fact, cultivated. Pyaung was no fool either, and he in turn fostered the notion—using it now and then to impose some plainly unpalatable assignment. The mere mention of a very great, remote, and invisible chief sufficed to cow these simple hill folk and to snuff out flickers of rebellion. So the ghost of Fitz, the cream of Western corruption, would haunt their dreams from time to time in the form of a majestic, omnipotent being whose will was law.

Mu bowed, yet Sanders read the reluctance behind his consent. He must have been hoping to receive the command himself, a job for which Sanders thought him imcompetent. He was about to walk away in silence when piercing cries rose from the corner where the critically injured were lying. He stopped and shook his head. "Three dead at

178

east, tomorrow; Mu is certain," he said. "What should be done?"

"I'll see what I can do to help them," said Butler, getting up.

He returned in a few moments and picked up Sanders's pack containing the heroin which was doled out to him every night as agreed. "May I?"

The sergeant looked on in silence. Butler took out the little packets. There were ten left, one for each day the trip was scheduled to last. Setting aside eight, he returned the other two to the pack. "In case of another mishap."

Dumfounded, Sanders began to protest. Butler's voice took on a sarcastic edge. "Don't worry, I know how to give injections. I've had plenty of practice at it."

He took the hypodermic needle reserved exclusively for his own use and walked away. Mu stood watching the scene, forgetting all about leaving. Like the rest of the soldiers, he knew of Butler's habit and what the packet meant to an addict. The two men couldn't see him in the dark, but imagined him crouching among the wounded. Gradually the moans faded away. A profound silence hovered over the camp when Butler returned. In the shadows, Sanders guessed, every single soldier had witnessed the performance.

"What about yourself?" he asked him.

"I don't need it any more," Butler replied, "I'm detoxified."

Mu, the Shan warrior, peered at him curiously in silence. He simply bowed and touched one hand to his cap in an odd salute, half-military, half-Chinese Mandarin.

He spoke once more, addressing Sanders in the Shan tongue while nodding his head approvingly. "The soldiers will obey the new chief. Mu pledges this."

13

FITZ WAS IN agony after receiving Wong's message giving
an abbreviated account of the ambush. The fact that the
incident had ended on a relatively happy note only partly
restored his peace of mind. He had projected a ten-percent
loss, as Sanders thought he would, and even with a higher
percentage the operation would pay its way royally. But a
third of the journey still stretched ahead, and now the
elimination of his two key men spelled disaster. It left only
that fellow Butler whom Wong had recommended to take
command of the expedition at Sanders's suggestion. This
new development, which conflicted with all his carefully
laid plans, struck him instantly as sheer folly. He discussed
the matter with Herrick.

"How can I place the responsibility for billions of dollars on a man who was shut up in a laboratory and gained no
experience or knowledge of the country and the pirates
who live there—who has no sense of leadership and can't
even handle a gun—and who's an addict in the bargain?"

"You have no choice," Herrick pointed out.

Fitz had to agree. There was no one else to lead the
march. He blamed his own oversight for allowing this to
happen.

"Now read Wong's message again. It seems to say that

Butler conducted himself more than honorably. Showed decisiveness and bravery. Apparently he's learned to hang onto a rifle and use it."

Once again, Fitz read Wong's account which relayed Sanders's comments. The answer was inescapable: the organization owed a tremendous debt of gratitude to one of its members. Without further delay, he sent off word to Rangoon confirming Butler's promotion to commander-in-chief.

Stephens was no less upset to hear of the attack. While his agents in Thailand scurried about gathering somewhat conflicting scraps of information hour by hour, he hung on tenterhooks for several days, fearful that the cargo had been stolen and scattered all over Southeast Asia. A more accurate, factual report finally brought him some comfort; but while it lifted his hopes, it also contained information so incredible as to revive all his doubts.

On the heels of their rout (a relative rout considering the plunder they had acquired), the Lahus, awed by the lightning shift in the battle owing to a single white man's initiative, could not seem to hold their tongues. The tales they spilled reached all the way to Thailand and allowed narcotics agents to reconstruct both phases of the skirmish. Butler (the third man was plainly the one in question—the description didn't fit the others) was extolled as a giant, a hero, a knight in shining armor at whose hands it had been an honor to suffer defeat. Even with allowances for the Oriental imagination and for obvious exaggerations and inconsistencies, there was still enough meat in the story to astound people, who, like Stephens, were familiar with the man's past.

A final report which reached him two days later informed Stephens that, in all likelihood, Butler was the man

now heading the expedition. After reading it over twice, h
gave up trying to fathom the nonsense on his own. Havin
had few occasions to consult Dr. Edmund lately, and wit
Allen covering an assignment on the West Coast, Stephen
went straight to the psychiatrist's office, hoping to hea
some rational comments, and, eventually, some helpful ad
vice.

"First of all, Doctor, do you recognize this man?"

After a brief exchange of greetings, Stephens re
sponded to the doctor's searching glance by setting befor
him the composite sketch received from Thailand a fev
weeks earlier. Edmund didn't hesitate.

"It's Butler, Stephens, John Butler. The former ser
viceman we talked about at length one evening—the addic
I treated at several different times, never successfully, I'n
sorry to say. If I remember correctly, you thought you migh
have to pry into his affairs one day, though not for the same
reasons as I. So now the day has come?"

"It sure has," Stephens muttered. "But are you positive
it's he?"

"Absolutely, and I ought to know what he looks like
It's he all right—with slight variations, that is: his eyes are
more alert, his jaw more determined."

"No sketch is as truthful as a photograph."

"True. His cheeks are a bit fuller, too. He looks heal
thier than when he was in my clinic."

"Fresh air," Stephens muttered resentfully.

"But I'm dead certain it's he. I gather you've become
seriously interested in him. The last I heard, he was going
the way of all drug addicts. What can I do for you? Or fo
him?"

182

"For me, first, Doctor!" Stephens exclaimed in an oddly plaintive voice. "For me, I'd like to get an impartial diagnosis, to know whether all this work of mine with gangsters and junkies has got me to the point of promoting and endorsing fairy tales?"

"I don't think so," the psychiatrist answered matter-of-factly. "You don't display the usual symptoms of my patients. I would merely observe that you seem to be under great emotional strain."

"You said it! Now let's talk about him. Listen, Doctor, this chicken-hearted, lazy good-for-nothing, this hardened addict, this seedy character with no guts, according to your description. . ."

"I never went *that* far," the doctor protested. "I'll admit that I was pessimistic as to where he was heading; still, at one time, I noted certain singular, interesting traits about him that might have led one to hope. . ."

"Damn all this prudence and reserve!" Stephens exploded, venting his frustration over recent developments. "Let me tell you the latest facts, which we at the Bureau are at a total loss to explain. Because this sad sack, this weak-kneed worm, exhibited the most astounding bravery in a land of savages—the name of which I'm not at liberty to mention—where, though moral standards differ from ours, the fiercest bandits know the meaning of courage. What do you say to that?"

He gave a brief account of the skirmish. The doctor listened attentively, one eyebrow arched, interested as much by the facts as by the agitation of a man ordinarily as poised and dispassionate as Stephens, who was used to dealing with highly unusual matters.

"So that's the story, Doctor, and what I really want to know, for my own peace of mind, is whether you think he'll

go on behaving this way, whether he's capable o
maintaining—please God, for a few days more!—this vital
ity and courage."

"I certainly do not," Edmund replied, shaking hi
head. "As I see it, he could only have behaved that wa
under the influence of a stiffer dose of narcotics. He actec
in a fit of feverish excitement. This happens occasionally
an overdose can result in a criminal act, suicide, or, rare
still, some phenomenal deed of reckless courage. Personal
ly, I've never encountered such a case, but I know the
exist. After all, Stephens, the name of the poison is heroin
there has to be a reason for it. Yes, a touch of madness, a
flash of impetuous temerity, the same kind of emotion tha
heavy drinkers sometimes experience before slipping bac
into a stupor. I imagine he'll have to pay dearly for it; h
must have paid a price already, a dreadful state of depres
sion."

"And here I expected reassurance from you!" Stephen
explained, throwing up his hand in dismay. "Don't you un
derstand that he's the only one left to bring the expeditio
safely through? Two others who could be relied on—whon
I could rely on—are out of the picture. What will happen t
the cargo with that miserable addict in charge?"

He was just as anxious as Sanders and Fitz for th
shipment to arrive intact. One thought, however, comforte
him. "That's not all, Doctor; he's already proved how per
severing he can be."

Stephens related how Butler had slaved for months t
learn chemistry and then achieved miracles according t
standards of the drug underworld. "Perseverance and in
dustry, Doctor, that's what did it. No impetuous fit of any
thing. Perseverence, grinding away day in and day out.
know, because his teacher, who's sort of a silly, trustin
soul, told me about it after she'd tutored him for months.'

184

"A woman in his life?"

"The one I mentioned to you once before. Yes, she was his mistress, but. . ."

"I told you that a woman can exert a strong influence on these unfortunate persons, can even effect a lasting cure. I've known of several such cases. Quite commonplace."

"Commonplace! But he's not cured, Doctor," Stephens snapped impatiently. "I have it from an unimpeachable source that he took drugs regularly out there, every day. The Shans nicknamed him something that means 'addict' or 'junkie'. Today, though, I'll bet they've raised him to heroic status: 'the fearless, blameless junkie'. Oh boy, I can just imagine! And you're wrong to think the girl meant anything to him. I know better; I've got proof. He dropped her flat with hardly a word of explanation the moment he was able to walk on his own two feet—I mean when he knew enough chemistry to be able to manufacture his confounded drug."

"Lust for gain, then; I don't see what else it could be," the doctor replied, shrugging his shoulders. "A sudden interest in money which could have developed rapidly into a passion. It did not cure his addiction, but kept it under control. Just another all too common case."

The sour pout on Dr. Edmund's lip conveyed his thoughts on such matters. "I presume they're paying him well for his services," he commented indifferently.

"I imagine so, but you never know about those people. The drug world is a world apart. The ones who deserve it don't always make the money. Or maybe he isn't so exceptional after all? Is that your final diagnosis, Doctor, a lust for gain?"

"I can't see any other explanation."

Stephens went away unsatisfied. The doctor paused to reflect a moment, then shook his head vigorously as if to drive such petty concerns from his mind. He couldn't do it,

which seemed to annoy him. Stephens's frustration probably was beginning to rub off on him. As he continued
thinking, the doctor began to feel that the patient in question might indeed possess personality traits that lay outside
his knowledge and experience. Sullenly, reluctantly, he
trudged into his library and began to reexamine his files on
Butler.

14

THE SALWEEN COMPLETED its metamorphosis in the last lap of its seaward journey. Tibet's threadlike stream, the turbulent crystal torrent exploding into cascades and churning rapids in the Shan States, had broadened into an immense river, subdued and sedate, whose waters began to reflect the ocher tints of rice paddies when the harvest is done and a long dry spell sets in. A few boats, sampans and small junks, signaled the plain's proximity. The bracing air of the highlands yielded to the sticky sultriness of Lower Burma. The caravan could still progress half-hidden among the last barren, desolate foothills; but on the right bank, which was flatter, planted fields—the first sign of civilization—began to appear.

The men sensed the change; soldiers and muleteers alike seemed loath to push forward. Used to braving danger in the mountains, they felt apprehension towards the vague, uncertain perils of the plain, their closeness to towns and villages. Even the animals were skittish. More than once, Mu approached Butler to ask anxiously if they ought to keep going much longer in the same direction. Butler mustered all his authority as leader of the expedition to reassure Mu and his men and to urge them forward.

Not to be overlooked was the fact that the trip seemed

to be drawing to a happy end. Having been spared further mishaps since the Lahu ambush, the soldiers unanimously ascribed this heaven-sent blessing to the stature of their new leader, to his bravery, and to his favor in the eyes of the gods. This interpretation was not so farfetched after all. In fact, as Stephens supposed, the legend of Butler was taking shape, spreading from Burma to Thailand. Though they still lusted after the treasure, not a single pirate band dared to challenge such an adversary, and the caravan, now inviolable, made its way peacefully under the protective wing of his virtues. He kept his word and took no more drugs. The fumes of glory, filling his nostrils like incense at each bend in the path, added a euphoric thrill to the sense of his new responsibilities, maintaining him in a permanent state of lucid rapture.

His smile reassured Mu, whom he had befriended. The trip was nearly over. The next lap, to be staged under cover of darkness, would be the last. Afterwards, the Shans could return to their mountains. Mu hastened to pass the word along to his men whose pace quickened accordingly.

The caravan left the foothills on a path that descended to the Salween. Butler took the lead, acting as guide. The night was clear, the trail not too hard to follow. He knew it by heart from having pored over a detailed map that Wong had sent to Sanders. Every mound, every hillock, every trickle of water—all precious landmarks, had been indicated.

He brought the column to a halt on a level stretch of ground, partly cleared of trees, overlooking the river. For the mules, it was the journey's end. He walked over to a cluster of three dead trees marked on the map and found, at the base of one, an iron stake, barely visible, driven deep into the ground: signal number one. He breathed easier. Despite final assurances from Rangoon the day before, he hadn't been able to stifle a nagging fear that the junk might fail to appear at the rendezvous and plunge them into a crisis.

He looked at his watch, approached the edge of the strip, and beamed prearranged signals with his flashlight. The reply came back almost instantly. He flushed with pride; momentarily, the exaltation of success knocked the breath out of him. He had brought the expedition through safely—a trek unprecedented in the narcotic traffic annals and which promised to become as legendary as his record in the laboratory.

The rest of the operation progressed rapidly and silently. Having received instructions in advance, each man knew exactly what to do and not a second was lost. While Butler followed a trail down to the river, soldiers and muleteers unloaded the cargo. Arriving at the water's edge, he saw the junk anchored some twenty yards out and flashed a second signal. Two sampans pulled away from the junk and rowed ashore. Wong was in one of them. He had left the snug comfort of his Rangoon bungalow for one night to personally supervise the operation. They hardly spoke before the loading began. Even now the soldiers were coming down the trail, carrying sacks on their backs and piling them noiselessly in the sampans which began shuttling back and forth between the shore and the junk.

Only then did Wong and Butler exchange a few whispers, with Butler confirming certain details that Wong already knew.

"A ten percent loss," he concluded.

"Reasonable, Mr. Butler," Wong replied, "there are bound to be losses in any operation of this kind."

"And nearly the same loss of men."

"Not too bad either. You can't make an omelette without breaking eggs, as they say in the West. How is Mr. Sanders?"

Sanders was in poor shape, suffering a raging fever from his infected wound. Soldiers were carrying his stretcher down to the bank; each jolt made him groan. Wong greeted him and sent him aboard the junk.

"I will take him to Rangoon with me. Tomorrow night he will be in the hospital; the doctor asks no questions. As for you, Mr. Butler, I have new instructions. Yes, a proposal for you."

Butler looked up. Since their meeting, he had been dying to ask about himself.

"Would you be willing to continue the trip aboard the junk and help deliver the cargo to a place I will name later?"

"Yes, gladly," Butler replied without further inquiry.

"Delighted. The higher-ups will be delighted, too. They are most appreciative of your valuable service to the organization, Mr. Butler. They know that the Burma expedition arrived safely because of you. That is why it is suggested that you conclude an operation in which you have distinguished yourself so brilliantly. They know no one more qualified than you to lead the next stage of the trip —until the cargo sails for the United States."

Never had Wong been so verbose. The truth was that Fitz's instructions concerning Butler specified that he be heaped with praise.

After analyzing the new situation created by the disablement of Sanders, who was supposed to escort the drug shipment to Malaya aboard the junk, Fitz had decided to entrust the mission and responsibility once again to Butler.

After all, someone reliable ought to be on hand to keep the crew in tow. The junk's captain knew this type of operation inside out, and, according to Wong, was dependable. But this time he would be carrying a priceless cargo. What guarantee of his loyalty would they have if he accidentally discovered the real contents of those presumed sacks of contraband rice and figured out their worth?

"Listen, Herrick, you don't assign billions of dollars to the tender care of a Chinese smuggler and his ruffian crew! For a week or more at that!" Fitz had protested, plunging into one of the many fits of despair that seemed to claim him as time passed. "Sanders was ideal for the job, not afraid to get what he wanted—by force, if necessary. So far, Butler has replaced him very adequately. Well, let him continue. Right now it's absolutely essential to have one of our own people in Malaya, too."

Herrick agreed. Butler was as good as anyone, and probably better than most.

"I think I'm beginning to discover some very unusual qualities in this man who seemed so ordinary. A kind of mutation. Just think how far up he's come since he started working for us, Fitz. I'll bet he'll do anything he can to keep climbing."

"And eventually replace you, or even me?"

"Who knows? You don't frown on ambition, do you?"

"He hasn't reached that stage yet. For the moment, let's leave him in charge on land and in the water."

"May I suggest something, Fitz? You ought to let him know that you're pleased with his services."

"Do you really think so? I wouldn't want his head to swell from thinking he's indispensable."

"But he *is* indispensable, let's face it. And there are billions at stake, Fitz."

"You're right," Fitz admitted reluctantly.

"Believe me, I'm getting to know him better. To this type of fellow, the esteem of his superiors will act as a powerful incentive."

Consequently, the deep satisfaction and the congratulations conveyed by Wong from the high command had all the earmarks of a general's dispatch from the front, in which one of his officers was cited for outstanding bravery and promoted on the field of battle. Such tokens of esteem, Herrick felt, would mean more to Butler than the promise of a fat bonus, which Fitz insisted on mentioning also. Wong performed his task with all the tact of a man who weighs every word.

Herrick was not mistaken. Butler gobbled up the praise from his unknown chief and eagerly accepted the proposal. Before Wong's words, his pride in having successfully carried out a delicate mission had begun to turn to resentment at finding himself excluded from the rest of the operation and obliged to turn over the treasure to hired guards who lacked the faith and courage to protect it—attributes which only a heightened sense of duty can inspire.

Once the loading was finished, Wong and Butler spoke briefly with Mu. The lightened caravan prepared to return home over the same route, for the Shans were not eager to linger in the vicinity of the plain. Wong counted out the contract price for this last lap, in silver rupees, adding a few extra to compensate for the dead soldiers. Mu looked pleased, even more so when Butler reached out and gave him a hug; then the Shan bowed low and vanished into the night with his band.

As the two men boarded the junk, the captain made a bow to Butler which was a degree lower than it would have been for the ordinary white stranger. The moment he set foot on the deck, the crew fell silent, peering at him curiously from the shadows. Butler interpreted the attention as a tribute, and indeed this was no illusion. Even by then, his legend had drifted beyond the mountains, and tales of his exploits were being told in fishermen's huts and smugglers' shanties up and down the coast. Wong knew what it meant, too, and he smiled.

The captain ordered the anchor lifted, and, with the motor off, the junk began its silent voyage seaward, propelled by the current and favorable winds.

Standing on the deck, Butler observed for one last time the nocturnal aspect of this land where he had met undreamed-of thrills and adventure. On the right, the river bank was strung with flat rice paddies; while on the left, the blurred outlines of foothills could barely be seen. He looked back for a final glimpse of Burma's peaks, but they were swallowed up in darkness. Sighing, he turned around again.

After sailing twenty miles or so, the junk entered the Gulf of Martaban just before dawn. There, a sampan was lowered to take Sanders and Wong ashore with two bodyguards who would carry the stretcher to a waiting car. On the river, Wong had instructed Butler about the next stage of the operation and had told him whom to contact in Malaya—last stop before shipping the cargo to New York. Butler's role would end there. Wong gave him a passport stamped with the appropriate visas and the papers he would need to re-enter the United States.

Butler watched the sampan fade into the darkness. The last thing he saw was Sanders on his stretcher, waving feebly, two fingers raised in the victory salute. He smiled and repeated the sign as the junk rounded islets in the gulf and entered the open sea.

15

STEPHENS HAD PUT aside the map of Burma which was no longer of any use. Obsessed instead, now, with maritime cargo notices, he was poring over a roster of ship arrivals when Allen entered his office.

"They're expecting a load of rubber on the fifteenth of this month, sir, from that plantation in Malaya; a Japanese freighter that stopped in Penang is on its way now to New York. I believe that's the heroin."

"What makes you think so?" Stephens asked, smiling enigmatically.

"A whole series of things. They only get this large a shipment about once a month, and the dates coincide if you allow a week for the trip from Burma to Malaya, by junk I'm sure. Furthermore, there's no reason for them to continue stockpiling the stuff out there; as a matter of fact, I'll bet that after all their troubles, the bigwigs here are dying to get their hands on the drugs. Anxious to make a killing as soon as they can. And there's still another reason, sir."

"Yes?"

"Butler has turned up again in New York. He traveled under a different name, but I managed to trace his steps. I know he arrived on a plane that left Penang two days after the Japanese freighter sailed."

"And considering the vital role he seems to have assumed in the organization, you surmise that he waited to leave until the ship was gone and his job over."

"That's right, sir. So I think it's more than likely that the *Koshiki*—the name of the ship, sir—is carrying the cargo we're after."

"And I'm dead certain of it, Allen!" Triumphantly, Stephens shoved the roster of ship arrivals he had been poring over under his aide's nose. The *Koshiki* was underlined in red. Allen looked mortified.

"Well, in that case, sir, if you've got better intelligence sources. . ."

"Don't get angry. I just got the tip yesterday. Our agents set up a listening post right on the plantation; their information checks with yours. That monstrous load of poison is definitely on the high seas this very minute, bound for New York."

"The ship is due on the fifteenth, a week from today."

"Exactly a week. We've got 'em, Allen!" Stephens shouted exultantly, clenching his fists. "I want to move in at the destination—Fitz's factory. I suppose you've got information on it?"

"Here's a diagram of the set-up, sir, and one of the neighborhood, showing all routes of access. You can see that the buildings are surrounded by relatively dense woods; good cover for us—we'll serve them up a warm reception."

Stephens couldn't suppress his jubilation. "Easy as pie," he chuckled, rubbing his hands. "Child's play compared to the hours of spadework, the patience, the painstaking care that we. . . that *you*, especially, invested for nearly two years."

"I hope Customs doesn't pick over those bales of rubber more than usual," said Allen with a worried look.

The competition between the Narcotics Bureau and the Customs Service was well known, each agency so intent on thwarting its rival that their separate efforts sometimes resulted in a joint defeat. Stephens frowned. "Don't look for trouble, Allen. We've been lucky thus far. This infernal drug is arriving intact, or almost so. No, the Customs inspectors won't cut the ground from under us, I'm sure. I tell you—we've got them. It's just a matter of arranging a few things."

He proceeded to attend to these and placed a private call to the police to insure their co-operation. Turning once more to Allen, he asked, "What about Butler? You say he's back; what's he doing?"

"Nothing, sir. Leading a life of ease, going to the movies and the theater, hanging around libraries. I'm having him watched, of course. My agent tells me he's put on weight. And he's tanned—from the tropics, obviously. In a nutshell, he seems in good health, if that's what interests you, sir."

Stephens shrugged his shoulders: an instinctive response of exasperation to the mention of Butler's name. "That guy never ceases to amaze me," he grumbled. "Anyway, his job is over. Fitz won't need him anymore; I suppose he's given him a nice fat bonus that'll put him on easy street for the rest of his days. Have him watched in the meantime; we'll arrest him when we're through with the others—the big guns and the brain behind this—that's the one I want to nab red-handed."

16

FITZ COULD NOT resist the urge to witness the shipment's arrival at his factory. The whole operation was too momentous, too marvelously successful for him to miss being there in the flesh for its triumphant climax. His feat of systematic planning over a period of several years had compelled him to run enormous risks, to combine guile and audacity, and, in short, to mobilize all the talents of his organizing genius. Now at last, after months of agonized waiting, he could bask in the rapture of success.

Two of his associates stood next to him: the indispensable Herrick, and Briggs—competent manager of the tire factory, who was preparing now to exercise his abilities in another area. The trio made their way through the plant on what appeared to be a routine inspection of the various units. Nothing unusual about this: it wasn't the first such tour made by Fitz, as V.I.P. on the board of directors. Neither the foremen nor the workers objected when he stopped to inquire about this or that new process, proving his familiarity with production techniques by the type of questions he asked. Actually, prior to making these visits, he would memorize a statement furnished at his request by Briggs, for he was determined to uphold the credibility of his adopted image.

The plant's employees were totally unaware of the operation in progress on this particular morning, or the fact that the premises would be host to the largest stock of heroin ever assembled in the United States. Truck drivers and crews, dispatched to the docks to transport the merchandise, thought they were handling the ordinary bales of rubber that came in every month. Only Briggs and Summer, the chemical engineer in charge of research, were in on the secret. In that respect, Fitz's scheme was ingenious; he boasted about it, assuming it to be foolproof.

He glanced at his watch impatiently. "They ought to have finished the loading. In two hours the trucks will be here."

The three exchanged furtive glances. As they walked through the yard, Fitz unconsciously slapped the palm of his hand against a wooden bench where the night watchman sometimes sat. He was getting superstitious. Customs inspectors loomed as the final obstacle.

"Everything will be fine," Herrick assured him.

"Let's talk about something else, if you don't mind."

There was no cause for his nervousness. Things were progressing on schedule at the dock. The bales of rubber, resembling all the others that arrived routinely from Penang—which was not on the list of ports suspected of collaborating in the drug traffic—drew no attention from the Customs officials. The bales were loaded onto trucks by unsuspecting hands and driven off to the plant.

"How about in the Far East—did everything go smoothly there?" Briggs inquired in an attempt to break the uncomfortable silence.

"Almost without a hitch. The only losses, ten percent, occurred in the mountains of Burma. . . plus two of our best men put out of commission. Luckily, there was a replacement on hand who turned out be worth both the others.

Have you seen him, Herrick?"

"I saw him. He flew in two weeks ago after completing his final assignment as skillfully and tactfully as we expected. He confirmed that everything went like clockwork on the water and in Malaya. What a strange bird he is, Fitz. After a month and more of exhausting travel under the most uncomfortable, unhealthy, and downright perilous conditions, he's never looked better. And to top it off, when I offered to supply him with as much free heroin as he wanted, he smiled at me oddly and said it wasn't necessary. He doesn't use it anymore. He's cured. He told me so and I believe him."

"I do too," said Fitz pensively. "No drug addict could have acted the way he did. Very peculiar indeed. Whether or not it lasts, remains to be seen. No trouble aboard the junk?"

"None. He was ecstatic about the boat ride and described every little island they anchored at. A dream world, he called it—mangrove trees, long stretches of sandy, deserted beaches shaded by coconut trees. You know what I mean: tourist talk! Of course, he must have found it relaxing after the long trek on muleback. Still, he keeps coming out with weird remarks that flabbergast me, though I'm getting used to his peculiarities. He announced to me that at last his eyes are open to nature—I burst out laughing right in his face!"

"No trouble with the crew? A mixed batch of Chinese and Malays who aren't too fond of whites, from what Wong tells me."

"On the contrary, he, who used to be such a loner and so withdrawn, made some close friends among them, he told me. Unbelievable, but he insisted that they came to *trust* one another. Again one of his fancy expressions. In any event, no one on board got the bright idea of checking the cargo. They parted tearfully, after the sacks were unloaded in a dry creek where trucks came to pick them up. In the warehouse, too, everything went according to plan."

"I know. I had word from there."

In fact, there hadn't been a single problem in Malaya. The bales of rubber, molded around the heroin containers, then pressed and stamped, had been substituted for the other, insignificant, shipment, unknown to anyone save a few insiders. The cargo went aboard the Japanese freighter without incident, under the satisfied, albeit melancholy, eye of Butler who waited at the dock until the vessel reached the open sea.

Flanked by his two associates, Fitz ended his official inspection, playing out his role of corporate magnate without a false note. He walked over to a shed that was of special interest to him: the one destined to house the drug before its dispersion to various centers. The heavy door stood open to receive the trucks which could drive inside over a trench designed to simplify the unloading process.

"This," said Briggs, "is the shed where we keep the rubber used for experiments. For the past six months I've been storing a few bales here. Summer, our chemist, comes and takes whatever he needs for the actual research projects he's working on which are more or less confidential. No one will think it odd if he continues his work. The night watchman has no key, and I know how to keep him from bothering us when we have a shipment to make."

Fitz expressed satisfaction with these arrangements and with the superb electronic burglar alarm system. Nothing was to be left to accident and Fitz had insisted that the set-up provide total security. "The trucks should be here any minute," he said, glancing at his watch again.

His impatience simmered down, when, a few minutes later, he heard motors roaring on the road outside the plant. The guard opened the gate. The trucks entered the yard and drove straight toward the shed. A triumphant smile radiated from Fitz's face.

He had no time to enjoy his victory. From outside, came the throbbing of other motors and a series of shrill whistles. The smile froze into an anguished grimace, his cheeks turned ashen.

Stephens had based the size of his raiding-party on the size of the haul and the likelihood of resistance. Actually, neither Fitz nor his acolytes entertained the slightest expectation of putting up a fight. Rarely did they resort to violence and, then, only if they thought it would pay off which was not the case now. None of them carried a gun. After this stunning jolt, Fitz tried to gather his wits together and find a way out of the mess by denying the facts.

The astonished factory guard had never thought to close the gate. Two vans roared into the yard, one filled with police, the other with narcotics agents. Stephens, flanked by Allen and the police captain, strode over to the trio. Stephens identified himself and pointed to the shed where the delivery trucks had entered. "I have a search warrant."

Fitz was just opening his mouth to protest when shots rang out. A policeman collapsed on the ground.

17

Like fitz, butler could not resist the temptation to take part, at least as a spectator, in the triumphant epilogue to an odyssey whose cantos still lulled him in his dreams.

No one had slaved as hard as he to create the treasure. No one could have mustered such vigor and courage to defend it against hostile humans or the elements, to bring it safely from the ends of the earth, over mountains and seas, to the Promised Land. He could not divorce himself from the experience now. And just as his attachment to the hoard ballooned into a miser's blind, reckless passion, so had his sense of responsibility to it sharpened acutely in recent weeks. Fitz was only half-wrong to interpret this as the kind of budding ambition which one day might covet the leadership of his organization. Rather than genuine ambition, right now, Butler's emotions represented a sublimation of his professional integrity.

He had got to the point of feeling—far more intensely than the unknown persons running the organization—*morally* bound to guard the treasure and to trust no one else with its safety. He simply could not bring himself to fade into obscurity without first verifying that the treasure was inviolable. He kept imagining that in his absence some accident might happen, some last-minute emergency arise which he and only he could handle. And so, along with everyone else, he had been reading the shipping notices since his return. When the Japanese freighter's arrival date was published, he decided to attend (unannounced, since no one had invited him, much to his humiliation) the cargo's unloading and to escort it to its final destination.

The drug he had ceased to consume now diffused in his veins a rapture far more intoxicating than the injected poison. He seemed unable and unwilling to break free of his epic adventure. Without stopping to realize that dangers in this part of the world were different, and demanded different reactions from those in the mountains of Burma, he took out of hiding his M-16 carbine, a gift from Sanders which he had carried proudly throughout the trip, handled expertly, and refused to part with in Malaya. Even then he had had a premonition that it would come in handy one day. Without it he felt diminished, robbed of the symbol of his glorious metamorphosis. And so, despite the risk, he had succeeded in smuggling it, dismantled, through Customs, in his luggage. Before leaving on the last leg of his adventure, he hid it under a blanket in the new car he had bought on his return with the princely bonus Fitz had given him.

At the docks, he watched the cargo being unloaded, then jotted down the license numbers of the trucks and waited for them to clear Customs. The two vehicles emerged very shortly and he saw them drive out to the highway with the shipment of "rubber." Though the likelihood of any complications was minimal from this point on, he resolved to follow the heroin to the factory. He trailed it from afar, never losing sight of it for more than a few seconds, around the curves. Anyway, he knew the address because the bales were all ticketed.

The trucks branched off the highway onto a quiet side road, and stopped in front of an iron gate which creaked open on its hinges. Butler sighed wistfully; now the adventure was truly over. The rest of the operation: the dispersion, the distribution to pushers, and the sale of the drug, didn't concern or interest him in the least. He had just resigned himself to turning around and heading back to town, when the whistles blew, the police cars converged on the plant from all directions, and two of the patrol cars drove into the yard.

He sized up the situation and acted instantly. He had learned to make split-second decisions and had developed lightning reflexes in the land of opium. Stepping on the gas, he slipped into the yard behind the two patrol vans. No one noticed him in the excitement of the raid. While Stephens was identifying himself to Fitz, Butler drove into the shed where the two trucks had disappeared.

"Throw down your gun and surrender!"

Surprised by the gunfire, the police had ducked behind the posts of a building facing the shed, the entrance to which was now blocked by Butler's car. They caught sight of him, on and off in the shadows, perched atop the last truck, wedged between two bales of rubber, blasting away. A policeman returned the fire but missed. Stephens signaled for him to stop and called out again: "Throw down your gun and surrender! We're covering the only exit. You're trapped."

A sneer was his response. The notion struck Butler as preposterous. Stephens's words vaguely recalled a similar situation, back in the remote past, when someone threw down his rifle before the first shot was even fired. As if, today, the hero of the Shan States, whose name was idolized in every mountain hut, as if this gallant knight were about to throw down his sword and give himself up! It was so absurd that the sneer exploded into laughter.

To a third warning, he hurled back defiantly, "Come and get it!"

More volleys rang out; no one was hit. Stephens consulted the captain. He wanted Butler taken alive. And there was no way for him to escape; true to the warning, narcotics agents were covering the only exit. But escape didn't seem to be Butler's goal. Hadn't he walked into the trap with his eyes open? And why, for God's sake? Once again the man mystified him. But this was no time for psychologizing; they'd have to bring him to his knees.

The police captain hesitated. His squad was strong enough to wipe out the crackpot. A hail of fire at the entrance while a few men sneaked around the back of the shed—no, it wouldn't be hard. But if the fellow still refused to give himself up, they'd have to shoot him.

Yielding to Stephens's request, the captain sent for tear-gas grenades, which at least would enable them to subdue the crank. He had just given the order when a cloud of smoke gusted out of the shed, followed by flames.

The fire burned wildly. Butler had put a match to the gas tanks of his car and the trucks. The two drivers, whom he had held captive at gunpoint till then, dashed for the doorway and escaped; he made no effort to stop them. In a matter of seconds, the vehicles were flaming torches; the shed interior had lit up like a blazing hearth. Fire reached the bales. Black, nauseating smoke, typical of burning rubber, rose and gradually fanned out over the whole plant.

"Good God!" Stephens shouted, "we can't let. . ."

Butler, however, like an obstinate Cerberus, continued to block the entrance to the inferno. Inside, the heat grew scorching. He stood in the doorway, uncovered, his profile sharply etched against the flames. With his carbine pointed at the enemy, he blazed away at anything that moved behind the posts. Another man was hit. The police captain darted a questioning glance at Stephens who was in charge.

"We can't let the whole place burn down. Get it over with fast."

The captain shouted an order. Two volleys rang out. Butler staggered, hugged the gun tight against his chest, and, clutching it fast, pitched forward into the flames.

18

"THAT'S IT, DOCTOR. I've told you the whole story, assuming it would interest you because your former patient played a starring role."

With just this in mind, Dr. Edmund had invited Stephens and Allen to lunch after reading the final episode in the newspapers. Stephens, sensing that the psychiatrist was dying to know all about an affair of which he had only heard snatches, went out of his way to reconstruct the case, step by step, sometimes with Allen's assistance. He wound up his tale and lit a cigar.

"Besides, it's no secret anymore. Fitz's future is in the hands of the law. He won't wiggle out of this one and neither will his cohorts. Caught red-handed. The bulk of that monstrous mountain of heroin escaped the fire. My information proved to be right: enough to poison the whole country for a long time. An investigation of Fitz's private records has revealed fraudulent accounts and several secret codes proving that he's been involved in the drug traffic for years. So, the ring has been broken and the principals arrested both here and in the Far East. Sanders was nabbed in Thailand after he slipped across the border. I think he'll come out all right, though. His army record and a string of citations should stand in his favor. After all, he was only a

minor character and the poor guy had to have a leg ampu-
tated in Rangoon. For a man of action, that's the end of the
road and punishment enough, it seems to me. The Malayan
plantation manager is also behind bars. Only Wong managed to elude us."

"Wong?" the doctor repeated absently.

"I told you about him—the Chinese in Rangoon whom
we finally identified. Important man; too bad he got away.
We finally prodded the Burmese police into action after
endless delays, and they've just informed us that he had
flown the coop by the time they went to pick him up. I'll bet
the rascal was warned by his own spies on the police force
I'm sure he made enough money to pay them off. Probably
gone to China or somewhere else by now. Anyway, we've
lost him. Try to spot one Chinese among hundreds of mil
lions!"

"And Butler?"

Dr. Edmund listened impatiently to the end of the tale
He wasn't too interested in the persons whom Stephens
considered key figures.

"Butler? I told you how he died. A senseless act on his
part—we had no real evidence against him. Like the others
he was just an accessory. A good lawyer could have got him
off with a couple of years in jail, and when he got out he
could have picked up right where he left off... Say, I al
most forgot to tell you something, Doctor; this will surely
interest you—he was cured."

"Cured? You mean detoxified?"

"That's right, detoxified. Tell him, Allen."

Allen obligingly picked up the story. "Apparently, he
quit drugs, Doctor. After he died, I had his apartmen
searched; we gave it a thorough combing. Couldn't find a
trace of drugs or any of the usual apparatus—the hypoder

208

mic syringe and needles that no slave of heroin can do without. On top of that, the autopsy showed no sign of a recent injection."

"So don't tell me that he committed this suicidal act in a fit of wild-eyed exhilaration under the influence of drugs," Stephens interrupted.

"I didn't intend to. I've thought a good deal about the case since we last talked."

"The coroner's report shows that the last needlemarks are two or three months old."

"Two or three months old," Edmund murmured. "Now, according to the story you told me, that would mean around the time of the. . ."

"The clash with the Lahus, when his two companions were disabled and circumstances forced him to lead the expedition, to assume enormous responsibilities."

"Forced by circumstance to assume responsibilities," the doctor muttered. "But suppose he assumed them of his own free will?"

Stephens thought for a moment before answering. "I'm no expert in psychology, Doctor," he said at last, "but I think we see eye to eye and I'm flattered."

"Great!" the doctor exclaimed with sudden animation. "I always misjudged that fellow. What could have changed him so? Love of money? No, not that; I took for granted that he was subject to certain influences which, in fact, never affected him at all. As I've often told you, some of these addicts are exceptional cases that elude standard diagnosis. That man was never destined to follow the beaten track. He went astray; or more aptly, he backtracked—like an eddy in a river off a headland which breaks away from the mainstream and starts to flow upstream. Countercurrents, Stephens!"

The two narcotics agents eyed him with surprise, especially Stephens who knew him well and had never heard him talk this way. He must have been over-excited.

"So, you've got an explanation now for his paradoxical behavior?"

"I've got several, a whole chain of them. But the first link is so simple and so strange that you're likely to dismiss it."

"Simple and strange?"

"They're not incompatible," Edmund assured him. "Read Poe again."

"I do from time to time."

"And read Conrad too. One of us—I forget whether it was you or I—compared him once to Lord Jim."

"I'm sure it was you, Doctor, and I think I know what you're driving at. But that still doesn't satisfy me."

"All right then, read Kipling," the doctor thundered, his eyes glowing as if under the spell of a mystic revelation. "Read *The Day's Work*, about the sanctity of one's daily task, the love of a good worker for his job. Haven't you ever experienced that kind of passion? How about you, Allen, when you spend night after night trailing a suspect? What do you say?"

"Nothing, Doctor," the young agent replied prudently, detecting a flicker of resentment on Stephens's brow. "Perhaps, I ought to point out to you. . ."

But Edmund was in no mood for a lecture. He interrupted, cheeks flushed with excitement. "Do you remember our last talk, Stephens? You were telling me that he displayed amazing patience and determination to absorb what that girl was teaching him. Right away I thought of a woman's influence. How blind I was! He simply had stumbled on a captivating occupation. Some people spend their

210

lives searching for one, Stephens; others lack the courage to search and die in disgust. But he was lucky enough to discover an occupation that suited him, as a member of that organization. . ."

"A criminal outfit, don't forget."

"It makes no difference. As a member of the ring, he suddenly became a conscientious worker—simple as that. It explains his rehabilitation, his moral regeneration. . ."

"Rehabilitation! Moral regeneration! Aren't you going a bit overboard, Doctor? You forget. . ."

"And don't you think it was better for him to live that kind of life for a few months—with a purpose, a hope, an ideal—instead of sinking further into the inferno of drug addiction? In that final tragedy you just described to me, don't you see that he was inspired by a sense of escaping forever the hateful torments of his youth? Don't you understand that he walked right into the bullets of your Hawkshaws to prove that the old man of his youth was really dead?"

"Keep your shirt on, Doctor!" Stephens burst out angrily. "You seem to want to bill as some kind of glorious transformation the commission of an odious crime. The sanctity of work well done! Good Lord, this sanctity could have poisoned thousands of young people."

"That's not my concern. I'm interested in curing patients. Sometimes I succeed; in his case, I failed. But he found his own cure, which physicians consider a healthy sign. He found it all by himself, without my help; I don't hold it against him."

"That wasn't the kind of advice you'd be likely to give him."

To Edmund, who was concentrating on his train of thought, the remark sounded faintly censorious, "Look, I *did* have something to do with it, you know," he observed with a tinge of pride, "at least let me go on thinking I did. Remember what I tell all of them: psychological rehabilitation depends entirely on you. Find an interest, something outside of yourself, and a supportive environment. So actually, he did follow my general advice."

"Besides being a brilliant doctor, I wonder sometimes if you're not also a hopeless cynic."

The psychiatrist acted as if he didn't hear the remark.

"That's how it all started. A unique case, Stephens. At last here's a man breaking away from the banality, the mediocrity that I find so depressing about most addicts. He's stepping out of the fog that used to vex me so. I see him standing in the daylight. He's hired first as a salesman—a menial job, but one that still requires him to use tact; to keep his wits about him in order to avoid arrest; to exercise some degree of psychological insight in testing for bona fide customers, and all this mental activity starts the wheels spinning. I see him hanging around dingy bars, feeling the thrill of a hunter stalking his prey, dreaming up new hiding places for his stuff—foolish schemes for the most part, but intellectually satisfying when they work. Self-approbation, Stephens, something he'd never known; it was a revelation. The joy of success, the first sign that, despite what his father and his teachers had drummed into his head, he really was good for something after all. Also, the pleasure of earning approval from his employers who must have possessed some rather astute insights. This Herrick, who took him in tow, seems to have been a very humane person—instinctively so, I would imagine."

"Basically you're right, Doctor, but this insight was no miraculous gift blooming in the heart of a gangster. Herrick was no thug."

Stephens informed him that Herrick had once held a prominent position, was well educated, and had earned several degrees.

"Which proves that it's a mistake to blindly run down professional training," Edmund commented coolly, "and that's a great comfort. Whatever you may think, the whole story is profoundly moral."

"Moral!" Stephens looked up helplessly, as if alerting some divine witness to a sacrilege, but the doctor cut him short.

"Herrick knew how to handle him, simple as that. I failed probably because I lacked his knowledge of certain types of people. Routine work to begin with, yes, but he dangled the promise of advancement, of inching up in the world, step by step. Social promotion—I can see it all. The girl was merely a catalyst."

"I always told you Bridget meant nothing to him."

"Bridget?" the doctor repeated, suddenly arching one eyebrow, that habit of his denoting either surprise or concentration. Stephens, a professional observer, took note of the twitch.

"Bridget is her first name, Bridget Dodge. Happen to know her?"

"Never heard of her," Edmund replied, shaking his head after a moment's hesitation. "Dodge or Ford, it's all the same to me. Anyway, we now agree that she's a person of no consequence."

This denial sounded a bit labored to Stephens, but he had no time to pursue the question for Edmund was speaking again.

"So now we find him raising himself up, exercising his mind. Soon comes the supreme reward—success, the radiant success of the craftsman, better still, of the artist

213

who attains unrivaled perfection. Enough to transform anyone's life. From that moment on, Stephens, he wa half-cured. Saved!"

"Saved? Go on, Doctor, I'm listening," Stephens mur mured, disarmed.

"Willing to sacrifice anything to preserve his work o art, he was ready to give up drugs—his paradise on earth— to give up his life."

As if plagued by a nagging thought, the doctor stoppe to ask, "By the way, that woman, that Bridget what's-her name, what kind of work did she do? What happened t her? Pure professional curiosity, you understand."

"I can answer your first question easily." Stephens ex plained Bridget's work in the laboratory. "What happene to her is something else, however. All I know is that sh quit the laboratory. Walked out in a huff. I was told the would have fired her if she hadn't made the first move. Ner vous breakdown, they said; her attitude became terribl sloppy, she wouldn't do any work, even the routine things and fought with all her associates. I gather that you're inter ested in her, Doctor."

"Not in the least," Edmund declared once again, wav ing the matter aside. "He's the only one I care about. A fascinating case. An example of detoxification that is uniqu in the medical annals; it will head my collection. Thanks fo all the details, Stephens."

Having finished their coffee and cigars, Stephens an Allen rose to leave. "Lots of work right now. The whole business isn't over yet for us. It has global ramifications tha will keep us hopping for weeks."

"Don't apologize," said the doctor, "I know what worl is. I have work to do at the clinic myself this afternoon *The Day's Work*, Stephens, *The Day's Work*!

"*The Day's Work*," Stephens repeated, smiling.

214

he doctor drove straight to his clinic in suburban New
'ork. His chauffeur noted that he never once opened his
mouth during the ride, though usually they exchanged triv-
al banter on the way. Edmund was deep in thought and
ppeared worried. As soon as the car drew up at the clinic's
entrance, he leaped out, neglecting to give the driver his
orders for the later part of the day. He rushed into his office
and called his secretary whose greeting went unacknowledged.

"We have someone leaving today, don't we?"

"Yes, Doctor. A woman heroin addict. She's been here
hree weeks."

"I've only seen her once. Dr. Lewis treated her, I be-
ieve. What's her name again?"

"Dodge," the secretary replied, "Bridget Dodge. She
used to work in a pharmacological laboratory. Quite a responsible job, I think. Probably that's where she got
hooked."

The doctor dropped his eyes, pausing long and
houghtfully while his secretary looked on, intrigued. At
ast he told her, "Have Dr. Lewis come in."

The moment the young doctor stepped through the
door, Edmund began to question him. "How is she? You
know the one I mean—your patient, the Dodge girl, Bridget
Dodge."

"She's doing all right physically," Lewis replied, taken
aback, for the clinic's director generally took very few cases
under his wing, leaving the bulk of the patients to his associates. "She went on drugs fairly recently. Too recently
for the heroin to have done organic damage. Her mental
condition is something else. Nervous breakdown, rejects
everything, especially her work."

215

"Her work?"

"That's what she told me. She used to be a chemist, you see. Well, it seems she's developed a loathing for chemistry and especially for the piles of administrative paper work she had to deal with. Couldn't stand the atmosphere of the place either. Classic symptoms. In a fit of disgust, she walked out."

"What did you advise her?"

"To seek out another, completely different kind of job."

"That's what you told her?" the doctor exclaimed in a strange voice, ill-suited to such an ordinary comment, Lewis thought.

"Yes, of course, and a different environment, too. The normal recommendations: find a source of interest. Didn't I say the right thing?"

"Yes, yes indeed," Edmund muttered absently. "A change of environment, a new atmosphere; yes, certainly. Will you send her in to me before she leaves? I'd like to see her."

"You think I didn't give her proper guidance?" the young doctor asked with marked annoyance.

"Nothing of the sort, my boy, You know I have complete confidence in you. A new interest surely is the answer. I simply want to repeat your advice to her. None of them hear it often enough."

Lewis left. Dr. Edmund returned to his silent musing until Bridget entered the room. She looked just the way he had imagined. He gazed affectionately at her.

"You wanted to see me, Doctor?"

"Yes. I understand you're leaving us today. I hope your stay hasn't been too unpleasant? Good. So tomorrow you'll be back in the world, a tough world." He paused, groping for words and hating himself for finding only clichés to offer her. "The treatment you've received here has been successful. Physically, I can see that you're in good health, but. . ." It was an effort for him to repeat the usual speech he delivered to patients at the close of the detoxification period. "The psychological cure is far more important, a matter of will power and patience. For each of us—and I know this from experience—somewhere on earth there is an oasis of serenity, of friendly understanding. You must hunt for it persistently and not be discouraged."

He recited this, on one note, like a litany, yet seemed absorbed in an entirely unrelated set of thoughts. He had the impression that she didn't undertand him and he felt like kicking himself for not being more persuasive.

"Dr. Lewis tells me you didn't like your profession. He advised you to try something new."

"I already quit," said Bridget. "That kind of advice is no help," she added resentfully, "chemistry is all I know."

"Then learn!" Suddenly he came to life. His tone changed as if, in his groping efforts to reach out to her, he finally found the right words and with them, the right accents. He went on speaking with mounting vigor. "Learn, Bridget! Something new: there lies your hope of salvation. Dr. Lewis couldn't give you better advice. If you don't like what you're doing, then do something else. Summon up all your strength to do it. It is absolutely essential for you to work at something that interests you—passionately. And to find it, don't shy away from the unfamiliar, understand? Hunt it out, as a matter of fact. Hunt it desperately, as if your life depended on it. Nothing is worse than routine, Bridget—banality, mediocrity. That, I know, is what threatens to trap you and drag you back in disgust to your addiction. I urge you, Bridget, don't be afraid to confront, to plunge blindly into perilous, fantastic adventures, even if. . ."

Carried away by his excitement, he uttered these last exhortations with both fists pummeling the table, his eyes darting fiery glances at invisible challengers. Now she was listening; the impact of his words finally had got through to her and she seemed shaken by their ring of fierce conviction.

"Even, Bridget, even if these adventures take you. . ."

He stopped in the middle of the sentence as a thought flitted across his mind. He arched one eyebrow a bit higher, glanced up at the sky beyond the bay window in his office, and murmured to himself, "If Stephens could hear me now!"